# THE BOY

## AT THE

# MUSEUM

a novel
by Tamera Lenz Muente

*TL Muente*

Tableaux Publishing
Erlanger, Kentucky

Tableaux Publishing
P.O. Box 18733
Erlanger, KY 41018

Publisher's Note: This is a work of fiction. Names, characters, places, and incidents are a product of the author's imagination or are used fictitiously. Locales and public names are sometimes used for atmospheric purposes. Any resemblance to actual people, living or dead, or to businesses, companies, events, institutions, or locales is completely coincidental.

The Boy at the Museum/Tamera Lenz Muente. — 1st ed.
ISBN 978-0-9915699-0-8

*to Kevin,*
*for believing in me*

*in memory of my Mom,*
*the first to believe in me*

Chapter 1
A Tough Lad

*Arthur Watson*

I had just enough pocket change to visit the museum on my way back to my rented room. The sun had already set, and a freezing mist gathered in the air as I reached the building's large wooden doors. A white-haired man stood between the two large columns that flanked the entrance. He greeted me and stretched out his hand, which was wrapped in a fingerless glove. I dropped my last three coins into his palm, and he pulled open the door.

"To the back and up the stairs," he grunted.

Dim lantern light sifted through the entrance hall. Proceeding toward the stairs, I peered at the displays along the way. On my left, large bones and jars filled with cloudy liquid and unrecognizable things lined up in rows on towers of shelves. To my right, a glass case held dozens of preserved birds, some lying on their backs with their pathetic legs curled in the air, others perched on branches as if still very much alive. As I moved closer to get a better look, in hurried the man from the front door.

"You're gonna miss the show," he said, gesturing down the hall.

I was not expecting a show, so I followed him to the staircase, my curiosity piqued. At the base of the stairs stood two ancient sculptures, both male torsos, one of which was missing its head. As I ascended the stairway, I saw the walls were hung with plaster reliefs, one a Roman battle, another a group of frolicking cherubs. At the top of the stairs, the second floor opened up into an immense space, its ornamented ceiling supported by rows of towering classical columns. A crowd gathered near the center of this grand hall, and as I grew closer, my nostrils filled with the scent of damp wool and grime. Women in long, full capes, men wearing top hats and dark jackets, and workers in dirty overalls who had completed their shifts at the mill jostled each other around a small elevated stage. Their voices echoed in the cavernous hall. The crowd hushed as a finely dressed man in a beaver top hat emerged from a nearby doorway carrying a boy in his arms. He stepped onto the stage and set the boy down. I loosened my scarf and craned my neck for a better view.

"Ladies and gentlemen," the man on stage began. "I am delighted you have braved the weather to witness this rare event. You see before you eight-year-old Enos Stutsman, an unfortunate lad born with a shocking monstrosity. At birth, Master Stutsman was deprived of the very instruments of locomotion God has granted us. He is essentially missing both legs. There are small stumps and sorts of feet, to be sure, but nothing that can support him physically. As you can see, the young man moves around much like an animal."

The boy leaned forward, placed his palms on the floor, hoisted his body, and swung his torso forward like a pendulum.

"I assure you, however," the man continued, "his wits have not been dulled. He is a smart boy who has been confined to his home these eight years without access to an education or the company of other children. His mother has taught him to read and write, educating him to the best of her ability with limited resources. He devours books and is very bright, and his mother wishes to build his intellectual faculties if he cannot rely on the physical. In short, she wishes to send him to school."

The man crouched and picked up the boy, placing him on one hip. "I thank you, dear friends, for the price of your tickets today will help fund his education." The crowd erupted in applause as the man walked from one end of the stage to the other with the boy in his arms.

After the man put him down again, Enos peered at the people staring at him. Directly before him stood a young woman with two children—the girl hid her face in her mother's skirt, and the boy leaned on the stage with his elbows. Enos locked eyes with him and suddenly lunged off the platform, knocking the boy to the ground. The woman shrieked, and the crowd parted to reveal the two boys thrashing on the floor. Enos scrambled on top of the boy and landed a few hard blows to his face. I rushed forward to pull him off, but he was remarkably strong and continued struggling. The man in the top hat

4 TAMERA LENZ MUENTE

jumped off the stage and helped me subdue him. The mother came to the aid of her son, who cried as she dabbed at his face with her handkerchief.

"I am sorry, very sorry, we will close early tonight. The boy's display will resume tomorrow at ten o'clock," the man apologized to the audience as he restrained Enos. The crowd murmured complaints as I helped haul the boy to the end of the hall and down the stairs.

"What were you thinking, Enos?" scolded the man.

"He was making fun of me! He made a face like this," said the boy, screwing his features into a grotesque mask.

The man introduced himself. "Joseph Dorfoy, proprietor of the museum," he said.

I must have appeared surprised. I had heard of the great Dorfoy even before I arrived in Cincinnati a few days earlier. This was my first chance to visit his famous Western Museum.

"Thank you for your help," he continued, as we led the boy to a windowless chamber that held only a bed, a side table, and a stove.

"Arthur Watson, at your service, sir," I replied. "He's a tough lad, isn't he?"

"Yes, and hardly accustomed to this environment. He'll adjust by week's end."

Enos moved to the bed in the corner. He didn't precisely walk or crawl but placed the palms of his hands on the floor in front of him, used his arms to support his weight, then swung the lower half of his body between them.

"Goodnight, Enos," called Dorfoy, shutting the door

behind him.

"Where are the boy's parents?" I asked.

"His mother did not have the means to travel," Dorfoy replied as we began walking slowly away from Enos's chamber.

"How long has he been here?"

"You are certainly full of questions, aren't you?" spat Dorfoy.

"Well, I..."

"He arrived yesterday, and he shall stay until every man, woman, and child in this city who wants to has paid their twenty-five cents to see him."

"How did you find him?"

"Again, with the questions."

"I just..."

"Since you're so curious, why don't you report to my office tomorrow morning? Let's say eight o'clock."

"Are you offering me work?"

"Just don't be late. Now, goodnight, Mr. Watson."

He motioned down the corridor in the direction of the entrance hall, which was now empty except for the shelves of specimens and rows of sculpture that lined the walls. I walked out the tall doors and onto the street. Freezing rain fell, making a ticking sound on the icy dirt road. I wrapped my scarf around my neck and buttoned my overcoat, but I hardly felt the cold while my head swam with thoughts of my strange encounter at the museum. Back at the boarding house, I lay in bed drifting in and out of sleep, confusing the murmurs of people coming and going with the sounds in my own dreams.

# Chapter 2
## A Great Natural Curiosity

*Arthur Watson*

I awoke to a racket outside and rose to look out the window, first wrapping the blanket tight around my shoulders. The fire in the stove had gone out, and the room was cold and damp. The purple glow of the winter sunrise illuminated the street just enough to reveal the silhouettes of a few men walking among low, rounded shapes. Pigs! There must have been a hundred of them. Their jostling bodies filled the entire width of the road as the men used long poles to drive them toward the slaughterhouse on the river. I sat back on the bed and thought, a job—I may have landed a job. I quickly pulled on my trousers and walked over to the washstand. Splashing the icy water on my face, I smoothed back my hair, grabbed my jacket, and headed down the hall to see about breakfast.

Mrs. Gibson, the proprietor of the boarding house, already bustled about, sweeping the floor of the breakfast room. A pot boiled on the stove as she turned to see me enter.

"You're up earlier than usual, Mr. Watson," she said as she poured me a cup of steaming coffee and set a plate of bread on the table before me.

"I'm seeing a man about a job today, I think," I said.

"You think? Whatever does that mean?"

"It's with Mr. Dorfoy, over at the museum."

Mrs. Gibson stood up straight and wiped her hands on her apron. "Oh, for heaven's sake. That explains it. My daughter's husband works for him. Dorfoy's an odd fellow."

"Odd? In what way?"

"Oh, forget I said anything. My son-in-law Hiram has made a decent living with him. To be sure, there is never a dull moment over there."

As Mrs. Gibson went about her business tidying up, I opened the daily gazette. Searching the advertisements, I came across this:

GREAT NATURAL CURIOSITY

at the

WESTERN MUSEUM.

*The citizens are informed that Enos Stutsman, a lad about 8 years of age, is now exhibiting at the above establishment, and from a conversation with Dr. Drake, who has visited and examined the boy, we learn that he does in fact present a very curious example of monstrosity.*

I pulled off a bit of bread and stuffed it in my mouth. After a description of the boy's peculiar condition, the advertisement stated that funds raised by his exhibition were to be applied to his education and support. I folded the paper, placed it under my arm, and ran back to my room to grab my hat. It was clear that Mr. Dorfoy would not wait, and it was nearly half past seven o'clock.

I reached the museum with some time to spare. The two-story, whitewashed building shone in the crisp early-morning light. A narrow dome flanked with small windows rose from the center of the roof, and two columns supported a porch off the second story above the entrance. Dorfoy stood above me there, leaning on the railing and smoking a cigar.

"You're early," he called down. "Come in. I will meet you at the door."

I walked up the few steps to the door and let myself in. Sunlight streamed through the windows and lit up the entrance hall, so I proceeded to look around. I paused at a long shelf which held a row of brightly colored, crystalline rocks. Above them sat a large brown object. When I moved closer, I saw that it was a bone, most likely from one of the animals of the past I had heard about. I had never seen one, so I slowly reached out my hand to touch it. Before my fingers grazed the surface, Dorfoy startled me with a cough. I quickly turned to face him. He was a stout man with a pinched expression like that of a mole. His tiny eyes squinted through a pair of spectacles, and his pointed nose jutted out above a small mouth and weak chin.

"So, I see you've found the mastodon bone. Lovely example. I am told it rivals the quality of those brought to Jefferson by Lewis and Clark from the salt lick just south of the Ohio."

"It's incredible," I replied. "I cannot imagine an animal this large."

Dorfoy laughed. "I don't have time to show you around now. Let's get down to business."

I followed him upstairs to the grand hall, where we had met under the strange circumstance the evening before. The stage stood empty, and I scanned the room, which was much easier to see in the daylight without the crowd blocking my view. The great columns rose to the ceiling, terminating in leafy medallions at the top. More display cases and shelves like those downstairs lined the walls, and several doorways led into smaller rooms around the perimeter.

"Come, Mr. Watson. You'll have plenty of time to browse later."

Dorfoy's office faced the second-story porch where he had stood when I arrived. Blue satin curtains were pulled over the windows, darkening the cramped room. Bookshelves lined one wall, and more books were piled on a table in the corner. I could scarcely make out the titles but noticed a few volumes of literature, philosophy, and science, in both English and French. His desk was cluttered with piles of papers, more books, and a mounted skeleton that appeared to be some kind of rodent. The room smelled musty, of old paper and ink. He pulled open one of the curtains to let the light in and told me to sit down. When I did, I noticed the skeleton's spine branched into two necks, each sprouting a complete skull. Dorfoy sat in the large leather chair across from me. He tilted his head back, looked down his nose through his spectacles, and studied me as if I were an oddity myself.

"I need you to look after the boy," he finally said.

"You mean the boy I met last night?" I asked.

"Yes, Master Stutsman. Just until his mother arrives. I don't have the time, and neither do my employees."

"But I don't know a thing about children."

"You have a way with him. That was obvious last night."

I shifted in my seat. "This isn't really what I had in mind. I don't think..."

Dorfoy leaned forward in his chair. "I will pay you well. More than some bank would pay you to sit and copy numbers into ledgers all day."

I thought for a moment. Filling ledgers was what I had imagined I'd be doing. But no prospects had shown themselves. I knew virtually no one in the city, save Mrs. Gibson, and if I didn't start making money soon, I would have to go back East. I certainly did not intend to show up on my parents' doorstep a failure.

"All right," I said. "I'll do it."

"Wonderful!" Dorfoy's face lit up. We stood and shook hands. "The boy is in his room, which you should remember from last evening. Now, if you will excuse me."

"Wait..." I interrupted.

"There's not much more I can tell you," he replied. "Just keep an eye on him till ten o'clock and then make sure he gets on stage. He may take a break at midday and for supper. The show ends at nine o'clock tonight." And

Dorfoy disappeared through a door at the back corner of his office.

I knocked on the boy's door five times. When he didn't answer, I pushed it open. A gray woolen blanket was balled up at the foot of the bed. On the floor sat a wooden tray holding an empty bowl and spoon. The walls were the color of ash, and the small lamp that stood on the bedside table had been extinguished. The only light came through the open doorway where I stood. Enos was not there.

My first impulse was to run back to catch Dorfoy, but I knew he would already be speeding away in his carriage. I stepped back into the hallway and looked to my right, then to my left. Nothing. The museum seemed quiet and empty, and I had less than two hours to find the boy. I could only pray he had not left the building.

Aside from the entrance hall, most of the first floor looked like storage rooms. I entered them one by one, looking behind wooden crates and under draped, dusty sheets, occasionally calling the boy's name. There were two rooms I had not yet searched, and I was about to give up when I heard a faint rapping. I ran down the hall toward the sound, which got louder as I approached the last room. The door was already open, and inside I found a room packed with wooden cabinets. Some had glass doors through which I could see empty jars similar to those in the grand hall. The knocking continued, but now it was accompanied by a muffled voice. It seemed to be coming from the back corner of the room. The sound grew louder as I hurried toward a low cabinet with double doors. When I reached it, I crouched down and slowly turned one of the handles. The door sprung open, and out fell Enos, sweating and panting.

"Dear God, boy!"

Enos lay on his back on the floor with his eyes closed, trying to catch his breath. "I've been calling for hours," he gasped.

I helped him sit up. "Enos, I'm Arthur Watson," I said. "I'll be taking care of you."

The boy couldn't have been more than two feet tall. In the light, and with his state much calmer than last evening, I saw that where his legs should have been were two misshapen, flipper-like feet on which he wore leather slippers. His arms were long and strong, perfectly formed, as was his torso. His tousled hair made him look as though he had just rolled out of bed.

"It made a perfect stagecoach until the door wouldn't open," the boy said.

His small size allowed him to fit easily inside the empty cabinet. I cringed when I thought about what might have happened had I not found him.

"Yes, indeed. A very good stagecoach," I replied. "And what for your horses?"

His eyes brightened. "Two great black steeds! And a driver, seated up high, cracking his whip as we drove through the wind, with thunder and lightning and pouring rain."

"My, you've had a busy morning."

He looked at me for a moment. "You're the man from

yesterday," said Enos. "I'm sorry I behaved badly."

"It's all right. Now, come on. We need to get you cleaned up for the day."

Enos rose, supporting himself with his arms. He was barely taller upright than when he sat on the floor. As we approached his room, he slowed down and came to a stop. He looked up at me and asked, "Do I have to sit on the platform again?"

"Yes. Mr. Dorfoy said we must be there by ten o'clock."

"But why?" he whined. "I just sit there. There's nothing to do. I won't do it again!"

My livelihood depended on getting this boy to do what Dorfoy expected. I crouched and looked him in the eyes. "Enos, you must do it. Your..."

"I won't do it!" he cried, and in a flash he was in his room, slamming the door. I was astonished at how quickly he could move.

"Enos," I said, opening the door. He had already hoisted himself onto the bed and pulled the blanket over his head.

"I won't. I won't! You can't make me. Where is my mama? She would never make me."

"Enos, please," I pleaded, kneeling next to the bed. "Your mother will be here in a few days," I said, even though I had no idea when she would actually arrive. "She will be pleased to hear you've been heeding your elders."

Still huddled under the blanket, Enos did not say a word but turned away from me to face the wall, "All right, then. I'll leave you," I said. I stood up and left the room, closing the door behind me.

First I walked casually, but then I quickened my steps. I did not want the boy to disappear before I returned. I headed back to the entrance hall, climbed the stairs, and let myself into Dorfoy's office. I scanned the bookshelves without really knowing what I sought. Then my eyes found the perfect volume, bound in red leather. I pulled the book out and returned to Enos's room.

"Enos," I said, pushing the door open. "I'm going to leave you something, and if you like it, you may bring it to the grand hall with you." I left the book on the floor and exited the room.

# Chapter 3
## The Grand Hall

*Arthur Watson*

At ten o'clock I waited in the grand hall, pacing the length of the great space several times. I began to think perhaps he could not make it up the long staircase by himself, but I continued to wait, my eyes trained on the stairs. Finally, I was relieved to see Enos emerge. As he drew near the stage, I saw he had placed the book in the waistband of his trousers. He didn't say a word, only looked at me and pulled himself up the steps onto the platform. He sat down in the middle and took out the book. I drew in a deep breath, exhaled, and nearly collapsed onto a bench near a large column.

The first visitors did not arrive until nearly eleven o'clock. I had dozed a bit, my head resting against the column, and awoke with a start to the voices of several middle-aged women. They spoke quickly, chattering away like clucking hens. I immediately sprang to my feet and looked toward the stage. Enos was still there, engrossed in his book. He was now lying on his stomach, propped up on his elbows with the volume open before him.

"Oh, my dear sweet child," one of the women said, her hand against her chest.

"How simply dreadful," said another.

"I would die, just die!"

"His poor mother must have seen something awful while with child," said another, in a lowered voice. "You know, in Boston there is a young woman who saw her husband mauled by dogs, and she gave birth to a boy covered with hair, with a black nose and the face of a wolf."

I heard the other women gasp, while one whispered, "Often times, it is the innocent child who pays for the sins of the parents."

I looked at Enos to gauge his reaction, hoping he did not hear these comments, but he simply continued reading. One of the women approached me. She was the oldest of the group, all sharp edges with a long, thin nose, hollow cheeks, and silver hair pulled back so tightly it seemed to stretch the corners of her eyes.

"Good day, Madam." I stood and bowed.

"Good day, Sir. My husband is a friend of Bishop Purcell, who has just opened the new St. Peter's Benevolent Society for children, and I could not avoid the chance to help an unfortunate boy. How wonderful our admission will go directly to his betterment and not into the hands of that eccentric Mr. Dorfoy."

I met her eyes and nodded. "Thank you, Ma'am."

She gave me a slight smile and turned to her friends. As if on cue, the group began their bustling movement. I was relieved when I saw the last of their heads disappear down the stairway.

Enos broke the silence that had fallen over the room. "You know, I've read this already. Mama gave it to me before we left for Uncle's farm."

"When did that happen?" I asked.

He sat up. "When I was seven, in the winter, when we left the city after Papa died. But I don't mind reading it again. I particularly like it when the monster escapes over the sea of ice, leaving Victor Frankenstein hopelessly behind."

"Why, yes. It is a good story." I wondered what kind of heartache this boy had suffered and where his mother was right now. "Would you like to get a bite to eat?" I asked, realizing I did not know where the kitchen was or who would even prepare our food.

Enos must have recognized my perplexed expression, because he put the book back into his waistband, lowered himself down the steps, and said, "I can take you to the dining room."

Enos led me to the first floor. Apparently I had missed several rooms on my search for Enos that day. He took me to what appeared to be a servants' dining room, furnished with a long, heavy table surrounded by mismatched wooden chairs. The room was clean and spare, but cramped. As Enos and I sat down, an old, stout woman emerged from a door at the back of the room.

"How wonderful to have someone else to cook for!" she exclaimed. She set a plate of bread on the table with her large, fleshy hands and disappeared again. She came back with some butter and a plate of pork. "Mr. Dorfoy rarely entertains and dines in his office almost every meal."

As Enos tore a piece of bread off the loaf, I noticed his hands were red and chapped. "Enos—your hands," I said.

"They're alright, really," he said, pulling them quickly under the table.

"Show them to me." Reluctantly, he placed his hands on the table, palms facing up. They were rough and calloused, and two of the knuckles on his right hand were raw and swollen.

"I've been exploring," he said.

"When?" I thought he had been sitting on that stage all day long.

"Well, I can't sleep in the morning, so I explore." His face lit up. "There is so much to see! Bones and insects and strange creatures in bottles. And even the Devil himself!" He spoke so quickly I could hardly keep up with him.

"The Devil!" I laughed. "Enos, you have such an imagination." He had, however, seen much more of this place than I had. I hadn't any time to look around since I arrived, and I was curious. I guessed he spoke of the famous Infernal Regions, which even my friends back home knew about.

"I will show you," he said. "Tonight, after my exhibition closes."

We ate quickly and returned to the grand hall. The space was empty when we got there, so I walked over to a group of shelves across from the stage. The midday sun streamed into the room through the large windows, and my footsteps echoed on the marble floor. As I approached the first shelf, I could finally see that the jars on it were filled with yellowish liquid. A strange animal specimen floated in each one, eyes closed, limbs held close to the body, as if in an embryonic state: a toad with its back pockmarked with holes from which tiny toads emerged, a young chicken with a malformed head growing where a wing should have been, a kitten with a third pair of legs emerging from its hips. These creatures looked tragic, waterlogged and limp, yet I couldn't take my eyes off them. I moved in closely to see every detail of their bodies, the claws and teeth, fur and feathers.

Enos was walking near a table on the other end of the room. I headed in his direction and picked him up so he could see. The table displayed not just one stuffed calf, its legs curled under its body, but rather two calves, joined at the buttocks, with six legs and two heads, one at each end. Matted and moth-eaten fur covered the specimen, which seemed to peer at us vacantly through cloudy glass eyes. Enos and I stared at it for a while, and I wondered how long it had lived and, if it had, how it walked around. The two heads must have wanted to go in opposite directions, threatening to tear its body in two. We were virtually alone in the museum, so we spent a good hour examining the oddities throughout with no visitors to interrupt us.

"Enos," I said as the boy returned to his position on the platform. "Please stay put. I will return shortly." He pulled out his book once again, and I went downstairs.

The entire place seemed quiet. I headed toward the entrance and stepped through the door. A blast of crisp, cold air hit my face. Down the street at the public landing, people busily hurried to and from the river. One steamboat was docked, and a man hauled a large trunk up a ramp onto its deck. Just then, a voice came from behind me.

"You must be Mr. Watson." I turned around to see the thin, shabby man who had taken my money the night before. Snowy hair wreathed his long, leathery face, and a thick, bristly moustache set off his crooked nose. "I'm Thomas. Watchin' the door, turnin' the tip."

"Turn the..."

"You know, talkin' to people, bringin' 'em in."

"Oh... yes. So, where is everyone?"

"Agh, they got that old negro woman over at Letton's. People'd much rather talk to the slave of Washington's father than see a bunch of two-headed, no-legged..."

"Washington's father? Why, that would make her, what, 150 years old?"

"I've seen 'er. She's all wrinkly, small and dark, with one tooth in 'er head and bony little hands. But, just you wait 'til tonight. Place starts hoppin' after 'bout eight o'clock. That's when Dante's Hell opens."

"The Regions?" I asked.

"Mmm," Thomas nodded his head. "Ain't you seen it yet?"

"No. I'm watching the boy. Haven't had a minute."

"Ain't open 'til after dark. You go tonight. Nothin' like it nowheres, not in these parts or anywhere."

"So I've heard. Say, is there anyone else around the museum during the day?"

"You got Ginny the maid, myself, and of course Mr. Powers."

"Powers?"

"Yessir, Mr. Powers, Dorfoy's wax man. He's always downstairs, tinkerin' in that workshop of his. He'll be in the Regions tonight, roamin' around. Nice young man, always sayin' hello and goodbye. Dorfoy's always havin' visitors. Important ones. Mrs. Trollope, Dr. Drake, Mr. Longworth..."

Now these were names I recognized. Mrs. Trollope! I had read the Englishwoman's acidic observations of Americans in the papers. Dr. Drake—the man mentioned in the advertisement about Enos. And, Mr. Longworth, the owner of the great, white house at the end of Fourth Street. Perhaps I had not made such a leap in accepting Dorfoy's offer after all. He was certainly well connected.

"Thomas," I nodded my head. "Nice making your acquaintance. I must get back to the boy."

"Likewise, Mr. Watson. Nice to meet you. See you at the Regions."

Enos and I whiled away the next few hours. He read, and I poked around the grand hall. Late in the day, Dorfoy emerged at the top of the staircase, holding his hat in his hand. "Mr. Watson! I trust Enos has not been too much trouble."

"On the contrary, Mr. Dorfoy," I replied, smiling toward Enos. "He has been very good company."

"Wonderful, wonderful! I pray, Mr. Watson, that you will join me for supper this evening after Enos has gone to bed."

I remembered the plans I had made with the boy. "Well, I was..."

"I simply will not accept your refusal!"

I glanced in Enos's direction. "I suppose that would be very fine," I replied. Enos frowned and cast his eyes down toward the book.

"What is that the boy is holding?" Dorfoy asked.

"I thought it difficult for a youngster to sit unoccupied all day, so I took the liberty of borrowing a book from your office."

"My office?" Dorfoy's face suddenly darkened.

"Yes. I thought..."

He stamped his foot. "You are not to step foot in my office without me!"

"I didn't know. I just..." I looked over at Enos, who watched our exchange with great interest.

"No matter," he said with a sudden smile. "We have much to discuss tonight. The boy can keep the book but do not take another." He turned to leave the room.

Nightfall came quickly, and with it, more visitors. Ginny busily lit the lamps that lined the hall, filling the air with the pungent odor of whale oil, as a crowd gathered around Enos. The people jostled to get closer to the stage. Enos, distracted now, was watching the crowd as they watched him. As if on cue, Dorfoy entered the room just as he had last night. He was dressed in his finery again, but it seemed he always dressed that way. He wore a high-collared white shirt with a white cravat around his neck, a gray vest, black coat, and tan trousers. He stepped onto the platform and removed his top hat before he spoke.

"Enos, come over here," he said. Looking tired, the boy moved toward Dorfoy. Several people gasped as they witnessed his unusual method of locomotion for the first time. "As you can see, the boy is quite mobile, much like a quadruped." He delivered the same speech as the previous evening, and afterwards people gawked at Enos and muttered to each other until Dorfoy reappeared at the back of the grand hall next to a set of double doors. An excitement filled the air as the crowd around Enos began to disperse, with most pushing toward Dorfoy.

I approached the stage. "It's nine o'clock," said Enos.

"I am very sorry I cannot accompany you tonight, Enos," I said. The boy said nothing. At the back of the room, Dorfoy flung open the double doors and people flooded inside. After the last few had disappeared into the dark corridor, Dorfoy glanced over at us before closing the doors behind them.

Back at Enos's room, Ginny had left a tray of food for his supper. "Enos, I promise we will go tomorrow evening," I said. Again, he remained silent. "Mr. Dorfoy is in charge, and I must do as he requests." We sat there quietly for a few moments. The boy's face looked faintly green in the flickering lamplight.

"Can you at least ask him when Mama is coming?"

I knocked on Dorfoy's office door. "Come in, come in," he said. I pushed the door open and saw him quickly close a large, leather scrapbook. He stood to greet me, gesturing toward a door in the back corner. He had removed his coat and vest and now wore only a loose white shirt tucked into his trousers, the sleeves rolled up to his elbows.

"Shall we?" he asked as we entered a small room attached to the office.

We sat down at a wooden table covered with a white cloth. Dorfoy had put on his spectacles, which reflected the lamp's flickering yellow flame in each lens. "Whiskey?" he asked, lifting the bottle to the glass that sat before me.

"Yes, thank you."

He poured for both of us, then raised his glass to me. "To the beginning of a wonderful business relationship."

I lifted my glass and took a sip.

Dorfoy sensed my confusion, and laughed. "My dear boy," he said, continuing to chuckle, "I am sorry we have not had time to discuss your responsibilities. How long have you been in Cincinnati?"

"Just a few days, sir. I arrived Thursday the last. The Gibsons are letting me a room."

"Ah, I knew it. I could see you were green to the gills."

"Then why hire me?"

"You weren't afraid of the boy. You jumped right in to break up that fight. I certainly cannot have squeamish people working for me."

"I was only doing what anyone would do. He could

have been seriously injured."

"More likely he could have seriously scrapped the other boy," Dorfoy chuckled.

Ginny brought a bottle of wine. "Catawba wine from Longworth's vineyards," said Dorfoy. She poured us two glasses, left the room, and returned with a tureen of onion soup, which she ladled into bowls. She served the food one course at a time—first the soup, next some roast duck, then a bit of cheese, and lastly a delicious pastry baked with cinnamon and pecans.

"Ginny has learned a bit of French cooking," Dorfoy beamed. "Americans eat their food all at once, like wolves. The French enjoy it slowly, savoring each flavor."

"Your name—it sounds like it could be French," I said, remembering the French books I spied on his shelves.

"You're very observant," he replied. "And your name, Mr. Watson?"

"My father is an Englishman. He came to Pennsylvania when he was about my age, built a home, started a farm, and met my mother."

"And you left the farm?"

"My brother is more suited to that life. I am more inclined toward the city. At least, I came here to see if I am. I guess you could say I wanted an adventure."

"And what do you think so far, Mr. Watson?"

"There is more to discover here than I ever imagined."

Dorfoy laughed again. His pale cheeks were growing pink from the wine. "Well, then. I shall give you your next assignment."

"What about Enos? Who will look after him?"

"His mother shall be here forthwith. You will keep watch over him until she arrives. And, when she does, I have a new task for you."

I leaned in closer. Dorfoy's eyes sparkled.

"I want you to pay a visit to Letton's. Investigate the place. Keep your ears and eyes open, and report to me everything you find."

He was speaking of the other museum in town. "So, you want me to spy on your competition?"

"Spy!" he spat. "Heavens, no. But you saw our empty halls today. Certainly, the Infernal Regions brings people in after dark, thanks be to Mr. Powers, but I need more visitors. You must do my research. Find out what the people crave, so I can deliver."

I nodded, listening intently.

"Dr. Drake opened the Western Museum with his lofty aspiration to make Cincinnati the scientific capital of the West—those were his words. Admirable, yes, but after a few years, things dried up. At first, people cared about Audubon's mounted birds and fish, the insects pinned to boards, the Egyptian heads and Roman vases and ancient bones. But soon they wanted surprises. They desired an escape from the drudgery of their lives. Drake hired me as one of his curators shortly before he was forced to sell. He could find no buyers for the collection, so he turned it over to me. Very soon, I discovered that the truths of natural science are not as attractive as the occasional errors of nature."

I found it hard to grasp Dorfoy's statement. It was

very late, and I was tired. "Thank you for the opportunity, Mr. Dorfoy. I must be going if I am to be back here early tomorrow." I drained my glass of the last drops of wine.

"Of course. I am pleased you are working for me, Mr. Watson."

Pushing my chair away from the table, I rose and left Dorfoy sitting in the waning lamplight and growing chill. Walking back to the boarding house, I rolled things over in my mind. I'd be receiving payment for visiting a museum? I couldn't believe my luck in procuring such easy and fascinating work. Yet something was odd about it. At that point, I had no idea how bizarre things would become.

# Chapter 4
## A Safe Arrival

*Arthur Watson*

I waded my way through another sea of hogs the next morning and arrived at the front door of the museum to see Thomas nailing a broadside to the door. "King of the Cannibal Islands" appeared in large black letters at the top, and beneath loomed a frightening head, hand-colored with red ink. It shot its menacing gaze from deep, dark eye sockets. Tattoos covered its pronounced cheekbones, and two tusks jutted from its mouth.

"So, is this today's offering?" I asked Thomas.

"G'morning, Mr. Watson," Thomas replied. "It's a cold one today." He turned and continued pounding the tacks into the door. When he finished, I skimmed over the rest of the poster. "Arrival... great curiosity... procured at immense expense... embalmed body... South Sea man eater...." I pushed the door open and walked inside, and at once I heard voices near the back of the entrance hall— Dorfoy's and another I did not recognize.

"This is an outrage," the other man shouted, his voice echoing. "When your audience discovers the truth, they will tear down this museum!" I could see his silhouette, his arms flailing in anger.

"Calm down, Mr. Powers." I recognized this voice as Dorfoy's. "It is harmless fun. You'll see."

"I certainly will not see. I am leaving, and I will not return until you have removed this hoax from view. I will not have my reputation tarnished by the false representation of my work." He turned abruptly and stormed past me out into the cold February morning air, slamming the door behind him.

"Good morning, Mr. Watson," called Dorfoy. "Mr. Powers and I were just discussing our new exhibit. It seems he has misunderstood my intentions."

"Exactly what are your intentions, Mr. Dorfoy?" I asked.

He walked over to me and put his arm around my shoulders, leading me into an adjacent room. "Sometimes, we must bend the truth slightly to give people what they want." He moved to the back of the room and pulled a cloth off what looked like a casket. "Behold, the Cannibal King!"

I gasped. A man's body lay inside a glass sarcophagus. He wore only a loincloth, and strange tattoos covered his dark skin. His fingers ended in long, claw-like fingernails. But his head was most terrifying. His broad face was a landscape of bulging cheekbones and cave-like eye sockets. His mouth stretched in a wide grimace, punctuated by two fangs the size of my thumbs. I immediately imagined him in the hot island sun, brandishing a spear and dancing around a fire that boiled a large pot brimming with human limbs.

"My God," I said. "How did you... where did you find him?"

"Mr. Powers is a genius," Dorfoy replied. "I received a shipment of waxworks from New Orleans last week, badly damaged, a real shame. The best was to be Lorenzo Dow, an irrepressible preacher recently deceased, but his face had been smashed beyond all recognition. Here lies before you Dow's head, with beard removed and face refashioned, placed upon another body. Powers's imagination is inimitable. He pulled two alligator teeth from my collection and appropriated the tattoos from a preserved New Guinea shrunken head."

"So, it is wax?" I leaned over the glass for a closer look. "Amazing! Truly amazing."

"I fear Mr. Powers thought I'd place this cannibal in the Regions or in another fantastical diorama. Let me ask you this—would you rather see a fake cannibal, Mr. Watson, or one in flesh and blood?"

"It is fake, and you are telling people it is real?"

"Does it matter? Real or unreal, they will experience an authentic emotion. Fear, amazement, repulsion, awe, something they are missing from their droning lives in the slaughterhouse or the mill. I excite children's imaginations and entertain the maids who care for them all day. Families come here together during the brief moments they have away from work and toil. I cannot, and will not, let them down, Mr. Watson." Dorfoy was quite convincing, yet between his words, quietly in the background, I swear I heard the jingle of coins.

When I went to fetch Enos, he was missing from his chamber once again. This time, I had expected as much. Why would a boy sit still in his room when tempted with such wonders to explore? I remembered a day when I was about Enos's age. It was a green, spring afternoon, the first of its kind that year, when the clouds move quickly across the bright sky and you feel everything coming to life. A fragrant breeze blew through the open windows of the schoolhouse where I sat spelling on my slate. That soft current of air caressed my face, and I knew I couldn't stay. When the teacher led us outside for a midday break, I hid behind the outhouse. When everyone was back inside, I stole off into the forest. Once hidden within the trees, I scampered as fast as I could down to the creek where I caught frogs in the cold water. I got a whipping from my parents that night, but I can still feel the water rushing against my calves and hear the wind moving the trees over my head.

I set out, as I had the morning before, to find Enos in time for the start of his exhibition. After poking my head in a few rooms on the lower level, I went upstairs, following a hunch. Sure enough, in a room off the grand hall, there was Enos. Fancy, painted banners that read "London," "Paris," "Istanbul," and "Rome" decorated the octagonal room, which was ringed with viewing holes. Enos had pulled a bench over to the wall, hoisted himself on top of it, and was looking into one of them. I walked up and peered into the hole next to him. A panorama of a European city was spread out before me. At the center stood a large cathedral capped with a mammoth dome.

To its right, a bell tower rose from the ground, surrounded by a maze of low buildings with tiled roofs. A word ran across the bottom of the picture.

"Florence," I said aloud. "Enos, you have found the cosmorama."

Each peephole opened up to a lovely vista of some faraway place. Next was Venice, with its canals and a man holding a long pole atop a gondola. How exotic, this city built on water. Then came Rome. A tall domed structure, which surely was the famed St. Peter's, stood in the distance, and two colonnades stretched around a piazza like embracing arms. In the center of the piazza, an obelisk topped with a cross stretched to the sky.

"Mr. Watson, come here!" He moved aside and let me take a peek.

"That is the Tower of London, Enos, the prison and palace of the English kings. It once housed a grand menagerie with animals from all corners of the world."

"You've been there?"

"Oh, no. I have never had the fortune to take the Grand Tour. But I have read of it."

"Papa and Mama took me to a menagerie once, in Philadelphia, before Papa fell ill. It was a hot summer day, and he carried me on his shoulders past the cages. The striped tiger was my favorite. He paced back and forth with his big pink tongue hanging out. At one moment, he turned and opened his great jaws between two of the bars of the cage, and his sharp white teeth flashed at us. Mama shrieked and fell back against Papa."

"Weren't you frightened?"

"No. He didn't want to eat us. He was just hot in his big orange and black coat. I wished I could open the cage and let him out so he could run back to his family, who must have missed him very much."

"Well, Enos, it is time. Shall we get to work?"

He pouted slightly. "Only if we can come back here later."

"Certainly."

"Oh dear! I've forgotten my book. Will you go back for it, Mr. Watson?"

"Yes, if you will go straight to the stage and wait for me."

I lifted Enos off the bench and placed him on the ground. He immediately headed to the door. I followed to be sure he got on the platform before I went downstairs. When I reached the boy's room, I found a small stack of books outside the entrance. Dorfoy, I thought, you must have a heart after all.

Enos and I spent the morning reading and chatting with the visitors who periodically came to see him. I heard myself saying, over and over, "Enos is a wonderful, bright boy." Most smiled kindly, and some said hello to the boy and asked about his reading, but inevitably they would turn to me and mutter, "What a shame," sucking air between their teeth, before leaving the room.

Shortly before noon, I heard the tapping of feet coming up the stairs. A small woman dressed in black appeared in the hall. When she saw Enos, she froze for a moment, and then her steps quickened. The boy looked up, and his brown eyes widened. He dropped his book and moved to the edge of the platform. "Mama!" he shouted.

"Enos!" the woman said breathlessly. She rushed over and swept him into her arms, covering his cheeks in kisses.

"I am sorry I couldn't come sooner," she said into his ear. "I will never send you away again, Enos, I promise." Tears streamed down her face as she held the boy tightly.

I stood up to greet her but quickly thrust my hands in my pockets and began to look around the hall. To say hello would interrupt their reunion. Just then, she caught my figure out of the corner of her eye.

"Beg pardon," she said awkwardly, as she placed Enos back onto the stage. She pulled out her handkerchief, dabbed at her eyes, adjusted her hat, and smoothed her skirt before walking over to me.

"That's Mr. Watson," Enos said from behind her. "He's been taking care of me."

"I'm Elizabeth Stutsman, Enos's mother."

"I guessed as much," I replied, laughing slightly as I bowed to her. "Arthur Watson. Pleased to make your acquaintance, Mrs. Stutsman."

She responded with a smile, and her eyes brightened. "Thank you for looking after my son. But where is Mr. Dorfoy?"

"He is very busy with the museum. He hired me two days ago to manage Enos."

"Oh, I see," she laughed. "He does require some managing."

Her pale skin glowed in the light streaming into the grand hall, and her cheeks were still pink from the cold wind outside. Wisps of almond-colored hair fell across her green eyes, still red-rimmed from crying. She tucked the locks back into her cap with a slender hand.

"You must be tired," I said. "Was your journey long?"

She sighed. "About two days' ride. The driver Mr. Dorfoy sent insisted on camping the night. I would have preferred to push through in case the weather turned." She rubbed her lower back, which was no doubt aching after her travels.

"I am glad you arrived safely. Enos could not stop asking about you."

"How I missed him!" She returned to her son and picked him up again. "I am so hungry, Enos. Shall we have a bite to eat?"

"Where are your things?" I asked. "Shall I fetch them and carry them to your room? I assume you will stay here with Enos?"

"I met Thomas outside, and he took my trunk. The maid has already arranged my lodgings next to Enos's room. I had to come upstairs to see my boy straight away," she said, planting another kiss on Enos's cheek.

The dining room was warm and smelled of cornbread. Enos hungrily grabbed at a piece, only to be stopped by his mother. "Enos—where are your manners?" He quickly pulled back his hand. "You know we must thank the Lord first."

"Sorry, Mama." He folded his hands and bowed his

head. I did the same. When we had finished, Enos tore into the bread as if he hadn't eaten in days.

"Mrs. Stutsman, take what you would like first. Surely you have not eaten properly since you left home," I said. She looked worn and thin, but smiled.

"Thank you, Mr. Watson." She filled her plate with steaming pork, sweet potatoes, and cornbread.

Ginny came by with a jug. "Whiskey, ma'am?"

"Oh, for heaven's sakes, no! I pray you have not been offering this to my son." She shot a hard glance at me. "Not in this town, where the Reverend Beecher himself preaches temperance!"

I swallowed hard and looked around the room, trying to avoid an answer. Of course Enos had drunk whiskey— there was not much else on the premises. "Mr. Watson," she demanded.

"I am sorry, Mrs. Stutsman. I was not aware of your position on drink."

"Well, I'd suggest you consider its effects. You should not drink it, either. Ginny, bring us something else."

A thick silence descended on the room and pressed down on us for some time.

Finally, I asked, "How long do you plan on staying?"

She looked surprised at my question and didn't answer immediately. Finally, she replied, "I do not plan to ever return to Indiana." She shifted in her chair and continued eating. Enos stopped chewing and looked at her without saying a word. "Enos, finish your food," she told him.

"So you will stay in Cincinnati?" I inquired.

She sighed. "I will not discuss it further, Mr. Watson."
I could see it was best not to press her.

Back in the grand hall, Enos took his place on the
platform. I offered Elizabeth the bench where I usually
sat and stood next to her. She watched the boy from
across the room, her eyes seemingly looking inward at
the same time.

"This is not where I hoped to be," she said, "watching
others stare at my son."

"I imagine it has been difficult for you."

"Enos has not been the difficulty, if that's what you
mean."

"Why, no, I didn't mean that at all."

"The minute he was born, I knew he was different but
felt the same as any mother feels for her child. My heart
filled with warmth when the midwife placed him on my
belly. Jacob—my husband—and I were proud of Enos
from the start. Of course, we feared that he would not be
accepted, but inside our home he was like any other boy.
We knew he was bright even before he began to speak.
He learned words quickly, then sentences, and was
naturally fascinated with everything. He would always
ask, what's this Mama? And I would tell him. I taught
him as much as I could. He could read by his fourth
birthday. Jacob would bring home the newspaper, and
Enos would read from it. But as he got older, it became
clear he should be in school. He should be around other
children. We knew this was nearly impossible, but it was
our dream."

"Where was this? Enos mentioned that you lived in a city."

"Yes, Philadelphia. Jacob was a cobbler there—his father established the shop when he came from Germany, and we lived upstairs. Enos was born in the same room that his father was born in twenty years before."

She stopped talking when we heard loud voices coming up the stairs. A raucous group of men emerged, unkempt and dirty. No doubt the five of them had come from the landing, taking a break between loads of cargo. They approached the stage, and Elizabeth looked at me anxiously.

"Look at the monster!" cried one of the men. The rest of them erupted in laughter. "Come here, boy. Let me pet you, little beast."

Approaching them, I could smell the stench of alcohol and tobacco on their breaths. I stood in front of them, tall and straight, trying to look bigger than I was. "You're upsetting the boy and his mother," I said. "I'm going to have to ask you to leave."

They burst out laughing again. One looked over my shoulder at Elizabeth. "You must be very proud of your son," he sneered. The others roared.

"You must leave immediately," I demanded, pointing toward the stairs. My heart pounded wildly, and blood rose up my neck into my head until I could hear it pumping in my ears.

"You must leave immediately," the man mocked. "Did you hear him, fellas?" He raised his arm and before I could dodge it, he landed a blow directly on the bridge of my nose.

"Mr. Watson. Mr. Watson!" I opened my eyes, startled to see Elizabeth crouching over me. Enos sat to my right, and Thomas stood to my left.

"What happened?"

"When that man punched you, Thomas was already on his way upstairs."

"Aye, I didn't trust those thugs," said Thomas. "Shouldn't have let 'em in, but Mr. Dorfoy hates it when I turn away payin' customers."

"Are you alright?" asked Enos. "Your nose is crooked."

"Certainly. I'm perfectly fine." I looked down and saw my blood-soaked shirt. How long had I been unconscious? I suddenly worried I had neglected my duties to Mr. Dorfoy, but when I tried to sit up, the room started spinning and I had to lie down again.

"Perhaps you should rest awhile," said Elizabeth. "Why don't you go to Enos's room until you feel better. Thomas, will you accompany him there?"

"Someone must stay with you and the boy," I said as Thomas began to help me up.

"Don't worry, sir," Thomas replied. "I won't let in any more of their kind." And with Thomas buoying my weight, we lumbered down the stairs.

# Chapter 5
# A Trustworthy Man

*Elizabeth Stutsman*

I must say I was shocked when I arrived in Cincinnati. I had read about the culture and refinement of this river town, yet few of the streets were paved. Freezing rain fell, melting when it hit the muddy ruts in the road. Rough men walked in and out of shops, and a terrible stench floated in the air. I realized soon it was the smell of a new life.

I knew the dangers of a woman traveling alone, but I was past the point of worry. My son had left nearly a week before, and I needed to join him soon. Mr. Dorfoy had assured me he would send his best drivers to claim both of us. So, on a Tuesday, the day Hans always went to town, I packed up my trunk and waited for the carriage. Weeks earlier I had pleaded with Hans to allow me to send Enos to an important doctor in Indianapolis.

"He may be able to help him," I stated.

Hans replied, "I don't see how. The boy's got no legs," and sank down into his chair, whiskey jug nearby.

"Because his condition is so unusual," I calmly continued, "the doctor has agreed to send a carriage and provide his services at no cost."

Hans's eyes darkened. "What did you offer him, Elizabeth?"

I thought for a moment. "Nothing."

"Don't lie!" He pounded the jug on the table, making me jump. "Man doesn't go around working for free."

"Nothing, I swear, Hans. It's in his own interest—to study someone like Enos would bring him great acclaim."

"I see. He wants to use the boy to make money. Money that should be ours."

"But he could help him. Get Enos those crutches he needs. He's of no use to you here on the farm. Please, just let me send him."

"Fine." And as he walked out of the room, he added, "but you're staying here. I need someone to cook for me."

Two weeks later, in the early morning hours of the coldest day so far this winter, I put Enos on a carriage. He cried, and I had to pry his arms from around my neck. His sobs grew from deep within, shaking his little body and mine as well. "Enos, you must trust me. I will join you soon," I whispered in his ear. In the growing light of dawn I tucked my warmest quilt around him and watched the carriage drive away—not to a doctor in Indianapolis, but to a museum in Cincinnati.

"Now maybe you'll get more work done around here without that little beggar distracting you all the time," grumbled Hans as I came back into the house. I continued past him and put the copper pot on the fire.

So, I am here, looking over a man I just met who lay unconscious on the floor of the museum. I used my handkerchief to dab as much blood off his face as I could, but he was covered with it. The nose bleeds so heavily. He was still, and his face looked so serene that I checked for the rise and fall of his chest to calm myself.

"Mama, how can I help him?" asked Enos.

"Just stay quiet. He'll wake up eventually."

"Ma'am," said Thomas, "Should I carry him downstairs?"

"No, no, Thomas. Let him lie here until he awakens."

"Good thing those roustabouts had work to get back to. I didn't want to have to hurt them."

"You were wonderful. Thank the Lord you came when you did."

On the floor between us, Arthur stirred.

"Mr. Watson. Mr. Watson!" I shook his shoulder.

"What happened?" He looked around, confused, and noticed the blood.

It was a fearsome sight when he fell at the hand of that awful man. I saw the fist connect with his face, and instantly Arthur's legs buckled. He collapsed to the floor right in front of Enos, who was still sitting on the stage. The men were laughing and slapping the back of the man who had dealt the blow. I suddenly felt their eyes on me, and although I wanted to go to my son, I took a step away from them, never losing sight of Enos.

"He started it," said one of the men, and again, the others laughed as they continued to approach me.

Just then, someone came up the stairs. "Don't you know how to behave in the presence of a lady?" a voice demanded. It was Thomas, the man who had helped me with my trunk.

"We're just havin' a little fun, old man."

"Go have your fun elsewheres," replied Thomas, pulling a pistol from his waistband.

"Come on, granddad, we ain't hurtin' nobody."

"Tell that to the man on the floor. Now, get outta here." He aimed the gun at them.

"Sure you know how to use that thing, old man?"

Thomas pointed the pistol toward the ceiling and pulled the trigger. The men winced, and I jumped, covering my head with my arms as a few chunks of plaster fell to the ground.

"Alright, alright." A few of the men put their hands out in front of them, palms facing Thomas, and slowly backed away. "We gotta get back to the landing. Boat leaves in a few."

As the men walked toward the stairs with Thomas training the barrel of the gun on them, one looked over his shoulder and winked, sending a shudder through me. Thomas followed them downstairs until they left the building. He then returned to help Arthur.

Now Arthur was awake, too dizzy to sit up. This man, several years younger than I, had so vexed me this afternoon but had listened as I spoke and tried to protect my son and me. He looked so small lying there in his crumpled coat and shirt, the center of his pale face punctuated by red. At that moment I sensed that Arthur Watson was a trustworthy man.

# Chapter 6
## First in Line

*Arthur Watson*

I woke up on my back in darkness. There was not even a bit of daylight filtering under the door. How long had I been asleep? I had agreed to visit Letton's Museum today, and now it would be much too late. As I sat up, I felt the dried blood stiffening my shirt. I couldn't go anywhere looking like this, and I wouldn't have time to return to the boarding house to change. Maybe Thomas could find me an extra shirt. Certainly Dorfoy had some lying around.

I lit the lamp, and saw the wide field of brownish red spread like a waterfall down my chest. As I sat on the edge of the bed, rubbing the bridge of my nose and marveling at the swelled knob that had grown there, someone knocked at the door.

"Mr. Watson, I trust you are well now?" It was Ginny.

"Yes, thank you. Feeling much better."

"I've brought you some clean clothes. I'll leave them here. Leave your shirt in the hall, and I will wash it for you." I heard her footsteps patter off.

I opened the door, and just as I thought, night had fallen. To the right, piled on the floor, was a shirt, a cravat, and a pair of trousers. When I bent over to pick them up, my head throbbed. I wouldn't need the pants, so I left them in the hall with my bloodied shirt. The clean, white shirt was of an older fashion, a bit wide, and the sleeves a little too long, but it would do underneath my jacket until mine was returned. Dorfoy would be back soon to do his little speech about Enos, so I quickly tied the cravat and headed to the grand hall.

Elizabeth sat there, concentrating on some needlework. Enos, in his customary posture since yesterday, was reading on the stage. It was one of the books that had been left outside his door.

"Good evening, Mrs. Stutsman."

"Mr. Watson," she said, setting the fabric on her skirt. "You've been asleep for hours. You seem much improved, but your nose looks ghastly."

"I assure you it is nothing. I hope that you and Enos are not too shaken from this afternoon."

"Oh, no, but thank you for your concern. We are quite well."

"What is that you're sewing?" I asked, looking at the small black bundle in her lap.

"A pair of trousers for Enos," she said, holding up the strangely shaped garment. "He wears them out so quickly, the seats of them can barely be mended."

"He is an active boy. Has he always been so?"

"Yes," she said with a smile, looking over at Enos. "Although he could not walk like other children, he could move around very quickly from a very young age. He perfected his method of locomotion by the time he was two years old. But I worry, now that his body is growing heavier, will his arms be able to carry all that weight?"

"I have noticed his hands," I replied. "They are raw and calloused."

"I tried to make him some mittens to wear, but he won't have them. He says they are slippery on floors, so he will only wear them outdoors in the winter."

Some people had gathered around the stage, and Elizabeth sighed and returned to her sewing.

I cleared my throat. "Mrs. Stutsman—I wonder if you are too tired to take in a bit of entertainment this evening?"

She looked up at me. "I am exhausted."

"It's just that yesterday I promised Enos I would accompany him to the Infernal Regions and at the last minute had to withdraw my offer. He was very disappointed."

"Infernal Regions? It sounds terrifying." She looked nervously at Enos.

"It is the attraction this museum is known for, far and wide. I have heard it is quite exhilarating."

"Well, the past several days have been difficult for Enos. I'm sure he could use a bit of cheering up."

"Wonderful. Mr. Dorfoy opens it at about nine o'clock. We'll go then. Shall I tell Enos?"

"Please do. He shall be ecstatic."

I walked over to the platform, and as I glanced back at Elizabeth, I could see she was watching me.

Dorfoy arrived as usual, stepping directly onto the

stage before even greeting us. After his performance he glided through the crowd to the back of the hall, where Elizabeth and I waited.

"Mr. Dorfoy," I said, "This is Mrs..."

"Ah, Mrs. Stutsman! I am pleased you have arrived safely."

She bowed her head to him, and it was obvious they had met before.

"Mr. Watson—why are you wearing Washington's shirt?"

"Washington's?"

"Our wax Washington wore that shirt on his deathbed, before I decided he should rather be crossing the Delaware." Dorfoy chuckled. "And your nose! What on Earth?"

I felt a heat rise in my cheeks. "We had a very trying day here, Mr. Dorfoy."

He leaned in toward me. "It's all right, my boy. Thomas told me all about it." Turning to Elizabeth, he took her hand in both of his. "I apologize, Mrs. Stutsman, for the trouble you have encountered here today. I assure you we will not let something like this happen again."

A restless group had already gathered at the double doors at the back of the hall. "Mr. Dorfoy," I said. "After such a day, we will be entering the Regions this evening."

"Heavens, do you feel up to it, Mrs. Stutsman? You must be exhausted after your long journey."

"Having a child often requires sacrifice, Mr. Dorfoy," she replied cheerily.

"Well, then, you must be first in line!"

# Chapter 7
## The Infernal Regions

*Elizabeth Stutsman*

Honestly, I was bone tired. All I wanted to do was fall into bed and drift off to sleep. My body felt heavy, and a dull pain throbbed behind my forehead. But Enos's eyes shone eagerly, and after what I put him through, I owed him a bit of fun. And I will admit I was a bit curious about the famous Infernal Regions. Even our minister back in Philadelphia had spoken about its moral qualities, and I had encountered many who could use some reform in that category. Mr. Dorfoy led us to the entrance, past those who were already waiting. I imagine most of them recognized Enos from the stage in the grand hall since no one argued as we moved to the front.

The double doors led to a narrow stairway. The space was close, filled with the pungent odor of burning whale oil from the few lamps that lit our way. Everyone was silent as we moved up the stairs, and when I saw the reddish glow at the top, my heart pounded in my chest. I was glad I had let Arthur carry Enos because the stairs were steep, and I began to lose my breath about halfway up. At the top, Mr. Dorfoy turned to the group. "Prepare to be mystified and terrified," he declared, pulling aside a heavy curtain to allow us to pass through.

A startling figure met us beyond the curtain. He wore a long, black cloak with a hood that obscured his face in shadow. He lit a torch and held it up to illuminate a sign above us: "Whoever enters here leaves hope behind." In the torchlight, I could see a skull and crossbones on the front of this man's robe and as he turned to the crowd, light glinted off his face, revealing a red lobster claw in place of his nose. I began to feel lightheaded and wondered exactly why I had agreed to do this. I swallowed hard and continued to follow Arthur and Enos.

Suffering souls in the throes of torture moaned and screamed in the darkness. A female figure sprang in front of our group, letting out a horrifying cry. I saw that her mouth did not move and realized she was made of wax. A huge snake dropped from the ceiling above us, and a three-headed dog—Cerberus, the guardian of the underworld—gnashed his shining white teeth. I focused on the back of Arthur's jacket as we moved through this Hell on Earth, my worries about Enos quelled by his delighted shrieks of laughter.

We passed between two skeletons holding a sign that said something about cherished limbs mouldering in the earth and the cold caresses of worms, a forboding welcome to the cave-like chamber that followed. Smoke filled the room, and unearthly sounds encircled us. Atop a craggy pile of boulders perched Lucifer himself, a red devil with glowing eyes and horns jutting from his head.

He held a pitchfork, his pointed tail flicked back and forth, and his head moved side to side, as if scanning the crowd for wicked souls. To his left was a world filled with fire—lava seemed to flow freely from the rocks, burying the tortured bodies writhing in the heat. A woman reached her arms upward, searching for some pitiable person to pull her from the inferno. To the Devil's right, all was cold. A man's face was paralyzed in a scream, his body half frozen in ice. I knew these figures were made of wax, yet the terror rose in me until I nearly fainted.

"Why doesn't that ice melt?" I heard a man next to me ask. I watched as he reached his hand through the iron fence that encircled the exhibit, presumably to feel if the ice was authentic. He immediately yelped, jumped back, and grabbed at his hand as a spark lit up the darkness— the barrier delivered a powerful jolt. Enos laughed at the man, who continued to rub his fingers, his eyes still wide with surprise. Then I saw a shadowy figure moving through the crowd toward the man, who was very much preoccupied with his electrocuted hand. It was the very same cloaked creature that had welcomed us near the entrance. As he sidled up to this unfortunate gentleman, the light from the exhibit shone into his hood. He noticed me watching and winked before leaning toward the oblivious man to bellow into his ear, "Do you smell sulphur?" I didn't know a person could jump so high! The crowd erupted in a hearty roar, and Enos and Arthur looked in my direction. I laughed until I could hardly breathe and I was certain this man would think twice in the future should he ever consider committing a moral indiscretion.

"Were you frightened at all, Enos?" I asked as we emerged from the dark stairway.

"Of course not, Mama. It was all in fun."

"The figures were truly lifelike. It was as if they were flesh and blood," remarked Arthur. "You may not have been scared, Enos, but I most surely was," he chuckled.

"I found it terrifying and exhilarating," I replied, "truly a wonder of our age. I should love to meet this Mr. Powers, who the handbill reports has accomplished this amazing feat. Figures that move and speak and appear to be made of skin and bone as if God himself had granted them life. How astonishing!"

We walked through the grand hall slowly as the crowd dispersed down the stairs toward the exit. Soon it was just the three of us.

"I have seen Mr. Powers and understand he has a workshop here in the museum. Perhaps we can pay him a visit," said Arthur. He continued to carry Enos, who had already fallen asleep on his shoulder. "Your son grows quite heavy when he sleeps."

"Yes, thank you for carrying him, Mr. Watson."

When we arrived at Enos's room, I lit a lamp and watched as Arthur carried Enos inside, laid him on his bed, and pulled the blankets over him. He grabbed his hat and coat, which he had left on a chair earlier when he used the room to rest. "Thank you for, should I say, an electrifying evening, Mrs. Stutsman," he joked. His nose had turned purple, and a slight bluish tint had developed under his left eye.

"No, thank you, Mr. Watson, for defending us this afternoon and for looking after Enos until I was able to join him. I see he truly enjoys your company."

"He is a remarkable boy," he said, as we stepped into the hall, gently closing the door so as not to wake Enos. "I bid you goodnight, Mrs. Stutsman."

"Yes, until tomorrow, Mr. Watson."

I watched him walk down the hall until he was out of sight.

I sat in the chair in the corner of Enos's room for a while, watching the outlines of his sleeping face in the dull lamplight. Every so often he wriggled beneath the blanket as if trying to sink deeper into its warmth, but mostly he lay there peaceful as a stone. The night chill was creeping in through the walls, and I knew I would need to get into my own bed soon. My room was right next door, and yet I hated to leave him. I thought of him alone in the carriage that brought him here. What kind of mother would do such a thing? Countless tragedies could have befallen him. He could have been lost in a snowstorm without food or drink, his tiny body freezing beneath the quilt I had wrapped around him. Indians could have attacked, carrying him off to live as one of their own or murdering him on the spot because they thought his strange appearance foretold evil spirits. Highwaymen looking for a quick penny could have intercepted the carriage. And since I had met Mr. Dorfoy only once, and so long ago, how could I have known his driver was trustworthy? He could have kidnapped Enos and sold him off to the highest bidder for some traveling sideshow. Jacob always feared our son would meet that fate, since so many others had. And look at us now.

"No son of mine will ever be gawked at," said Jacob when he had read the advertisement for the itinerant showman who had rolled into town with a wagon full of oddities. It was the first warm spring day of the year, the kind of day that beckons you to come outdoors after a long winter, so we left Enos with his grandmother that afternoon and strolled the several blocks to see the show. Banners flanked the public square, swaths of canvas hand-painted with "Trask's Traveling Museum," promising the impossible, the stupendous, the shocking. As we walked under one of the banners, a leathery, dark-skinned man wearing a turban collected twenty cents from Jacob for both our admissions. A large, blocky wagon stood in one corner of the square, its side opened like a giant armoire. Shelves that held bones, jars, and animal specimens filled the two open doors from top to bottom. An ancient sculpture head and a large, curved tusk sat on the roof of the wagon. In front, wooden crates formed a makeshift stage that was covered in a worn Turkish carpet. A general feeling of anticipation filled the air as fathers lifted children onto their shoulders and women talked giddily with each other. Jacob grabbed my hand and pulled me through the crowd into an empty space that was closer to the stage. A shabbily dressed man stepped down the ramp that stretched out of the back of the wagon.

"Welcome, fair citizens of Philadelphia. I am Mr. Trask, and what you will see today I guarantee will astound you." He gestured with his cane toward the shelves of curiosities. "The mysteries of nature will unfold before your very eyes. You will witness unfortunate individuals who have been imbued with peculiar conditions. All have been authenticated by a doctor to be real and unfabricated, but I ask you to judge with your own eyes." I looked around to see a rapt audience. No one said a word as Mr. Trask gave his presentation.

"First, meet Mr. Marlowe, the Living Skeleton." A tall man wearing only a loincloth walked out of the back of the wagon and proceeded onstage. The crowd gasped— he seemed nothing but skin and bone. The man's face resembled a skull, with sunken eye sockets and high, wide cheekbones. The tendons in his neck looked like tightly stretched rope. Thin bones ran from his chest to his shoulders, from which hung bony arms with elbows that jutted out like knots in a gnarled tree limb. He lifted one arm and gestured with his hand, showing off his fingers that were as skinny as sticks of chalk. He then placed his other hand on his side, drawing attention to his ribcage that curved like a basket around the hollow where his stomach should have been. He walked to the end of the stage on impossibly long legs that were set wide apart as if they dangled from the outer edges of his hips. How did they hold up his weight? As he turned around, his profile was as thin as a broom.

"Believe it or not," Mr. Trask continued, "Mr. Marlow's wife is a wonderful cook." The crowd laughed. "Would you like to meet her?"

A cheer erupted as a huge woman lumbered out of the wagon. She was the largest person I had ever seen. Mr. Trask took her hand and helped her onto the stage. I immediately, and a bit ashamedly, thought of the nursery rhyme I often sang to Enos when he would not eat his supper—Jack Sprat could eat no fat, his wife could eat no lean. I shook it out of my mind as this unfortunate woman, who could barely walk, proceeded to the end of the stage. Her hulking presence made the thin man look even ghastlier. She did not wear a fashionable dress for ladies, but wore sleeves that exposed the round rolls in her arms and pantaloons that ended just below her knees, revealing folds of fat that sank over her ankles. Her fingers looked like the pork sausages we bought from the butcher. She took her husband's hand, and he nodded and smiled at her. Together they turned and walked off the stage.

"Nature has made this next young woman not entirely whole. Meet Miss Cecilia Duncan."

A delicate girl, probably not older than fourteen or fifteen, stepped genteely from the back of the wagon. She wore a pink dress, its full skirt brushing the ground. The ruffled shoulders of the gown were pinned where her arms should have been. I looked at Jacob and could see in his eyes that he, like myself, was glad we had left Enos at home.

"Regardless of having been deprived of the use of hands, Miss Duncan has developed a talent for needlework." Mr. Trask brought a wooden chair to the stage, and the girl sat down. He then set a wicker basket at her feet. As her foot emerged from underneath her billowing skirt, I saw she did not wear shoes. She lifted her right foot into the basket, and with her toes brought out a piece of linen. The audience drew in their breath as she lifted the fabric all the way to her face and placed it into her mouth. She then reached back into the basket and pulled out a needle and thread with her left foot, grabbed the fabric once again with her right, and began stitching with her toes.

"I like to make floral embroidery," she said in a sweet, young voice, smiling as she looked down at her work. After a few minutes, she held up the fabric, which she had obviously been working on for some time, for it was already covered in pink roses, yellow daisies, and blue forget-me-nots fringed with green vines.

I awoke with a start, not realizing where I was. My heart beat quickly, and I took a few long, deep breaths to quiet it until I felt the chair beneath me and remembered I was in Enos's room. I could hear my son breathing, which calmed me considerably. As I leaned over to blow out the lamp, I knocked a tin cup off the bedside table and onto the floor, but Enos did not stir.

# Chapter 8
## Letton's Living Sea Dog

*Arthur Watson*

I arrived at the museum the next morning feeling groggy but ready to check on Enos and Elizabeth before a day of errands for Dorfoy. I had not slept much the night before, kept awake with thoughts of Elizabeth and Enos. My heart leaped when I saw her smile as we walked Enos to bed, but the sullenness she expressed earlier in the day still hung in the background like a distant fog. Why would a young woman come to the city alone? She showered her son with such affection—why would she allow him to be displayed as a curiosity?

"Mr. Watson!" Elizabeth was in a panic. She ran toward me, lifting her skirts off the ground, her heels clicking on the floor. "Enos is gone!" Her chest rose and fell as she tried to catch her breath.

I couldn't help but chuckle. "Calm down, Mrs. Stutsman." I put my hand on her shoulder. "He does this every morning. We'll find him snooping around somewhere."

"He's never run off like this before. I don't understand."

"I'm sure you don't live in an environment that is as interesting to a boy as this place. Come, let's look around. I assure you, he's here somewhere."

Rather than taking my usual route through the building, we headed immediately upstairs. "He's probably up here in one of the exhibits."

Elizabeth wrung her hands and glanced quickly around each apartment we entered, calling Enos's name repeatedly. No luck this time. We headed back downstairs, and after turning a few corners we finally heard hammering and voices echoing from down the hall. Elizabeth's steps quickened, and I hurried my pace to keep up.

Three large windows lined one wall of the high-ceilinged room, and early morning light streamed through, silhouetting two figures inside. After a moment, I realized it was Dorfoy and Thomas. Thomas held a crowbar and was working to open a large wooden crate. Dorfoy walked around the box giving orders.

"Try the sides first, Thomas," Dorfoy demanded.

"I've done that. They won't budge. We must get the lid off," replied Thomas.

"I'm telling you, Thomas. The sides first."

Thomas held up the iron bar. "Do you want to do it?"

Dorfoy huffed and began pacing back and forth.

"Maybe you should cut a hole so it can crawl out." A young boy's voice came from behind the crate.

"Enos!" shouted Elizabeth.

"Mrs. Stutsman. We didn't know you were there," said Dorfoy.

She ran over and picked up the boy. "Enos, you shouldn't run off like that without telling me. What are you doing here?"

"I couldn't sleep, and I heard Thomas out in the hall. He was lugging in this big crate, so I followed him. He said I could help."

"Agh, this damned crate!" said Thomas, hitting the box with the crowbar.

"Don't destroy it. Do you have any idea how much I paid for that thing?" said Dorfoy.

"What's inside?" I asked.

Just then, Thomas breached the crate's seal. The lid came off, pierced through at the edges with long nails. I then noticed the small holes punched throughout the sides of the box. As Dorfoy helped pull off the lid, a strange odor wafted out. Elizabeth covered her nose and mouth with her hand.

"Do you want to take a look for yourself?" asked Dorfoy.

"Let me see, let me see! Mama, take me over there."

I moved closer to the box and peered inside. The sawdust-filled bottom was shadowed by the tall sides of the crate. Finally, my eyes adjusted, and there it was: a thick, dark, coiled thing, with one end moving about like the head of a... snake! A massive, writhing, seething snake!

"Dear God!" I exclaimed.

"Isn't she a beauty?" shouted Dorfoy.

Elizabeth moved closer and looked inside. She let out a long, piercing shriek and jumped back. I went over and lifted up Enos so he could have a look.

"What is it?" he asked.

Dorfoy puffed out his chest. "It's an anaconda. All the way from the Amazon. Nothing like it has ever been seen here."

"Will it eat us?" asked Enos.

"Oh no, my dear boy," Dorfoy chuckled. "At least if it cannot get its body around you to squeeze the air from your lungs."

"Mr. Dorfoy—don't say such things!" Elizabeth interrupted.

"It will be quite safe behind glass. We will feed it rats."

"Live rats?"

"Enos—" Elizabeth said sharply. "Really, we must get you to work," she continued, and took the boy from me to place him on the ground.

"Mr. Watson, will you be coming with us?" he asked.

"Not today, Enos. I have work to do for Mr. Dorfoy. Your mother will keep you company, and before I leave I will bring you your books."

"Will we see you later?" Elizabeth asked.

"Yes, of course."

"If you need anything today, find Thomas or Ginny," offered Dorfoy. "They can get you whatever you need. Now, Mr. Watson, let us take a stroll."

The four of us walked out of the room, leaving Thomas behind to build the snake's cage. Elizabeth and Enos headed up the stairs to the grand hall where they would spend the next several hours.

"She's a fascinating woman, isn't she?" asked Dorfoy.

"She is very devoted to her son. At times she reminds me of my own mother when I was Enos's age. Of course, then I thought I was being smothered, not able to do as I pleased. But now I see that she only wanted to protect me."

"And you can only imagine what terrible things a boy like Enos would need protecting from. There are many enterprising men who will try to take advantage of unfortunate cases such as himself."

"But, why is she here? Why would she allow people to pay to look at him? I simply do not understand it."

"Are you that naïve, Mr. Watson? It's money. It's always money."

"You said that the money people paid for admission would support the boy's education."

"Once I hand the money over to Mrs. Stutsman, she will use it as she sees fit."

"Certainly she will use it for Enos. After all, he's really the one who has earned it."

"Again, Mr. Watson, I cannot control what Mrs. Stutsman does with the money."

I thought about this as we walked toward the entrance hall.

"Do you doubt Mrs. Stutsman's character?"

"Come, Mr. Watson. I've already seen the way you look at each other, and you've scarcely known her for a day. You do know she is years older than you, and a woman traveling alone could only be doing so out of desperation. You have hardly begun a career and have no home of your own, and the difficulties of raising a boy like Enos would be nearly insurmountable."

"On the contrary, sir. Enos is fiercely independent. He is remarkably intelligent and has an imagination well beyond mine as a youth."

"You saw his other side the night we met. The boy has a fiery temper, which will likely develop further as he grows. I fear he gets it from his mother."

I laughed this off. "Can you blame him? Would you not be occasionally frustrated if you had been deprived of what others take for granted? With the right guidance, which Mrs. Stutsman is so obviously capable of providing, I'm sure he will mature into a fine young man."

I sensed Dorfoy was perturbed with my argument. "You need to be aware, Mr. Watson, that what you do here is strictly professional. You must keep the personal separate from your work. I see how much you enjoy Enos, but you must remember that he will leave within a fortnight, and Mrs. Stutsman with him, and you will move on to a new assignment."

I nodded my head. "Absolutely, Mr. Dorfoy. You are worrying unnecessarily. As you said yourself, I have only known her for a day, and Enos just a little longer." I had been thinking about a way to return early to spend time with the two of them but now thought it best to wait until supper.

"Fine. Well, I'm happy you are free today to do some errands outside the museum. You need to see more of the city, my boy," he said, slapping me on the back.

Letton's Museum was a short walk from Dorfoy's, but I decided he was right—I needed to see more of the city. It was an unusually warm morning for February, so I detoured to explore. Besides, I didn't think Letton's would open before ten o'clock. I walked south on Main Street toward Front Street and the public landing. I could already see the sun, low in the sky, glinting off small chunks of ice floating in the river. I heard that sometimes the river would freeze solid and stop all traffic, bringing the city to a standstill, but not today. A sternwheeler had already pulled in, its two pillared decks encircling the boat like great white verandas. Roustabouts hauled cargo up and down the ramp, carrying kegs on their shoulders and pulling large crates with a rope. Nearby, a row of wagons waited to be loaded, the horses' breath puffing out clouds of steam in the morning air. A group of passengers, likely from St. Louis or New Orleans, had already disembarked from the vessel and looked around as if lost, until one of the gentlemen spotted a carriage and began shouting orders, motioning to one of the workmen to bring around their luggage.

I continued on past the shops that lined Front Street. In these tall, narrow buildings one could find almost every item made in Cincinnati or brought here on the river. Women strolled in and out of the soap and candle shop, men stood at the tobacconist or came and went from the taverns. A grocer's sign read, "Newly arrived— rice, pepper, molasses, sugar," all of which made my mouth water since I had not eaten much for breakfast. I reached a furniture shop and paused at the window to watch a man turn a table leg on a lathe. Next door, a woman sold wonderful fur hats, and I would have bought one had I the money. Up ahead, an awning stretched over the entrance to a grand hotel. Beneath, a disheveled old man in blackface strummed a banjo, his hands wrapped in rags to his fingertips. Further in the distance I could see steam rising from the flour mill, and all around me I heard the clopping of horses and the animated voices of men doing business. Dorfoy had certainly selected the best location for his museum, so near this hive of activity, the gateway for almost all visitors to the city. It was near ten o'clock now, so I headed back around the block toward Letton's.

A tall, narrow brick building housed Letton's Museum, a much smaller establishment than Dorfoy's. A young man greeted me at the door, and I placed a shiny quarter in the palm of his hand—Dorfoy had supplied me with money for admission and incidentals—and stepped up a few stairs into the entrance hall. The wide corridor was lined with ornately framed landscapes and cityscapes from around the world. Potted palms stood between each painting. At the end of the hall, ancient coins were mounted behind glass, flanked by two crumbling Roman portrait heads. A sign pointed me in the direction of a staircase toward the museum's newest exhibit.

Another man waited outside a room at the top of the stairs. For a nickel I purchased a pamphlet from him. I read the front page—"A Living Sea Dog. The first animal of its kind ever brought alive into the western country." There was no one else inside, as I had arrived soon after the museum opened, so I walked into the room, taking note of everything I saw. The middle of the room was fashioned into a large pen, complete with several platforms, a large zinc tub filled with water, and a walkway that encircled three sides of the exhibit, allowing visitors a close look at the creature. However, at this moment, there was no sea dog to be found, only straw scattered about and a fishy odor. I returned to the doorway and asked the man where the creature was, and he politely told me I must wait until some other visitors arrived, at which time the animal's keeper would bring it out. And so I waited. And waited. After about twenty minutes, a young woman with her chaperone walked in, and a few minutes later, three men. We all milled about restlessly until a door on the side wall opened, and a young man entered. He held a bucket from which he pulled a silvery fish. He held out the fish as he walked into the room backwards, making little coaxing noises. "Come on, come on," he encouraged. The spectators looked at each other skeptically, then back at this man who ridiculously begged the creature to enter the room. Finally, we heard a shuffling, flopping sound, and in it came.

It was the strangest thing I had ever seen. Its sleek skin was a dappled gray and black, and it supported itself on four flippers rather than legs. Its front appendages were strong enough to hold up its strong chest, which it stuck out proudly as it surveyed the room. Its head slightly resembled a dog's but with a more pointed snout and nearly imperceptible ears. Its eyes were clear, round, and dark, its long whiskers white and bristled. The creature used its front flippers to drag itself, and undulated like a fat inchworm as it propelled itself forward. As the man placed the fish in its mouth, I could see rows of sharp, white teeth. He led the sea dog onto one of the platforms, where it threw back its head and let out a strange, guttural bark.

I opened the pamphlet and learned that the animal's shiny skin was actually short, sleek hair and that its flippers ended in sharp claws, which I had not noticed. I looked back up, and the man called the creature toward the tub of water, into which it dove from the taller platform. Its head popped out of the water, and the man gave it another fish. The young woman and the older lady accompanying her laughed in delight. Although the tub was only about twice the length of the animal's body, the creature seemed at ease in the water, alternately dipping its head under and popping it back up again, the liquid rolling off effortlessly. The pamphlet explained that sea dogs were elegant, speedy swimmers that often play around ships at sea, and I imagined the creature and its family quickly gliding among the waves, happily chasing fish. The man called it again, and it pulled itself out of the water onto the lower platform. Although it could get around, its movement out of the water was clumsy and slow, and I felt a pang in my chest for this animal that would probably never again return to the sea. After watching the sea dog for a few more moments drag its plump body through the straw from one platform to another, I stuffed the pamphlet into my coat pocket to take back to Dorfoy. I had not seen the entire museum yet, but I had an urgent errand to run, one that Dorfoy had not instructed me to carry out.

# Chapter 9
## The Illustrious Dr. Drake

*Arthur Watson*

On my way to Letton's that morning, I had happened by Dr. Daniel Drake's office, and now I hurried back there. Dr. Drake's office stood near Fourth and Vine streets, the most fashionable quarter of the city. As I walked away from the east end of town, the air became clearer as the stench of the slaughterhouses began to lift. Paved walks lined the street, along which stood two- and three-story townhouses behind elegant wrought-iron fences. Smoke rose from their chimneys, filling the air with the warm scent of burning wood. A church clock tower rose into the sky at the end of the block, and its bells chimed twelve o'clock just as I approached the doctor's office. With some luck I hoped to catch Dr. Drake at his office during a midday break.

I had never been inside a doctor's office before. My only contact with doctors had been back at our family farm, where the doctor would visit only in the most dire of circumstances, of which I clearly recall only one. When I was about ten, my younger brother, Harold, fell ill. His slight, hacking cough quickly grew into a deep, hoarse one. We shared a bed, and at night his coughing never stopped. His raspy breathing kept me up all night, and I was angry each morning when I had to rise early, barely able to keep my eyes open while I gathered eggs from the chickens before I went off to school. Harold seemed to be fine during the day except for occasional bouts of coughing, so I saw the situation as more of an annoyance than anything else. Then, one night, not long after we had gone to bed, I woke up sweating beneath our quilt and realized that the heat was coming from Harold. He was burning up. The blankets around him were damp, but his skin was dry and hot to the touch. I tried to rouse him, but he would not wake up. He was only seven, and his small body seemed even smaller then. My heart pounded as I flew out of bed and ran to my parents' room. My mother was the first to spring from bed. "Arthur, fetch Dr. Adams," she yelled as she ran to our room. As I went to the door, I looked back to see my father entering our room behind her, and heard my youngest sister crying.

It was a short distance into town, so rather than spending the time to saddle our horse, I ran. I sprinted as fast as my feet could carry me through the chilly late autumn evening. A full moon silhouetted the skeletons of trees and lit my way, and leaves blew over the road. When I reached the Adams' home, panting and sweating, I pounded on the door until Dr. Adams answered. He put on his spectacles as he opened the door, and his eyes looked puffy and half-closed. Two words had barely come out of my mouth before he saw the panic in my eyes, disappeared for just a moment, and returned wearing trousers and a coat, his leather satchel in hand.

We arrived to see my father pacing in the front room. My three sisters sat quietly at the dining table. My mother was in our bedroom wringing a cloth into a basin of water and applying it to Harold's forehead. She had pushed his sleeves up above his elbows and opened his nightshirt to expose his chest.

"He won't cool down," she said to the doctor as we walked in, looking at him with her eyes swollen and red from crying.

"Arthur, go and take care of your sisters," Dr. Adams said. And he shut the door behind me.

"What could possibly be happening in there," said my father, still pacing.

"Father, why don't you sit down?" I asked. "Harry will be alright. It's only a cough." I consoled myself with this idea. My father paused for a moment and looked at me, and his eyes told me that this was more than just a cough. He started walking again, from the hearth to the window and back again. I got up to get a small rag doll that lay on the floor and took it to my youngest sister, Catherine. She grabbed it tight to her chest, stuck her thumb in her mouth, and slouched back in her chair. My other two sisters had fallen asleep, their heads resting on the table upon their folded arms. I don't remember falling asleep but awoke to our bedroom door opening and Dr. Adams carrying out a bowl of water reddened with blood.

"He's through the worst of it," Dr. Adams said. My mother stood beside him looking more exhausted than I had ever seen her. My father rushed to her side and put his arm around her, and I saw her weight lean into him. "He's very fortunate. You'll need to give him his medicine daily and keep a close eye on him until he gets his strength back. He is very lucky to be alive." My mother turned her head into my father's chest, and her body began to shake with sobbing.

Harold spent the next several days in bed with my mother catering to his every need. Each night when my father returned from the fields, he sat with Harold until my mother called him to supper. By week's end, Harold was begging to explore the forest with me, but he was not allowed. Another week went by before my mother let him walk the long route to school with me. All winter she demanded I walk him home immediately after school each day. He sat in our house while I played on the frozen creek or ran around the snowy forest. I stole him away one day when huge snowflakes fell, and we threw snowballs at each other beneath the trees blanketed with white, but when we returned I received a licking, so I didn't try that again. It wasn't until spring that Harold was allowed to play outside again, but my mother and father continued to coddle him and keep him closer than the rest of us.

I rapped at Dr. Drake's door with the brass knocker, which was cold to the touch. I waited a moment, and just as I began to reach for it again, a young man opened the door. He stuck his head out into the cold.

"May I help you?" he asked, his eyes squinting against

the noontime sunlight.

"I'd like to speak with Dr. Drake if he is available."

"He is out making house calls, but I expect him to return shortly. Won't you come in?"

I stepped over the threshold and surveyed the room. It resembled a parlor with upholstered chairs and small tables standing on a large woven carpet. A fire roared in the hearth, keeping the room comfortable despite the cold outside.

"You are the only one waiting for the doctor, so please take a seat. He'll be with you as soon as he arrives." He sat down at a desk and resumed reading a large volume. I could see drawings of the human body on the pages, which he scrutinized with great attention. He was, of course, one of Dr. Drake's medical students.

I waited for perhaps an hour, a bit worried that I would upset Dorfoy by not working. But this was equally, if not more, important in my mind. Finally, Dr. Drake entered through the front door. As he removed his wool cape and top hat, he approached his student, who picked up a pen and waited for instructions.

"William, please make a note that the laudanum seems to be helping Mrs. Todd's ailment. I will check on her again next week. I set the Cary boy's broken arm— God knows why he was climbing an ice-covered tree in the middle of winter—but his father couldn't afford payment. Follow up with him in a few days. Mr. Strauss's headaches have returned, and if resting for a few days does not diminish them, I suggested he come here for treatment. Oh, and I've scheduled a lecture at the Natural

History Society for next Thursday."

The boy wrote feverishly as Dr. Drake dictated to him. When he finished, the doctor asked, "Any news here?"

"A gentleman is here to see you," he replied, motioning to where I sat.

"Good day to you, sir," Dr. Drake said as he walked over to me. I stood to greet him.

"Pleased to make your acquaintance, doctor. Arthur Watson," I said as I held my hand out.

He shook my hand. "Likewise, Mr. Watson. Now, what can I do for you today? I have just a few moments before my next appointment arrives. Why don't we step inside my office?"

He led me down a hallway to a room furnished with a large, dark wooden desk. Bookshelves and anatomical charts lined the walls. He gestured to a chair in front of the desk and sat down to consider me. His hair was wavy and a bit messy. Thick sideburns ended at his strong chin. His heavy eyebrows set off deep, brown eyes that looked directly at me when he talked, and when he listened, a furrow formed between his eyebrows.

"So, what brings you here, Mr. Watson? If you're here to see me about your nose, it looks broken and perhaps slightly dislocated."

I had completely forgotten about my bruised face and broken nose. "Oh, thank you, sir, but my nose feels quite fine."

"Hmm. You're not familiar to me—you must be new in town."

"Yes, doctor. I arrived several days ago in search of work. Mr. Dorfoy hired me to assist him at the museum."

"Ah, my dear friend Joseph. We have quite a history, the two of us." He leaned back in his chair and folded his hands over his stomach.

"Yes, he's told me a bit about you."

"Probably that I couldn't make a go at the museum business," he laughed.

"Oh, no," I replied, worried I had insulted him.

"Honestly, Mr. Watson. I give Joseph full credit for saving that institution, whether or not I agree with what he's done with the place. But, enough about that. What can I help you with?"

"Well, it is somewhat related to Mr. Dorfoy. I read in the daily gazette that you examined a boy named Enos Stutsman who is currently at the museum."

"Yes, I saw the boy a few days ago. Bright young lad with an unfortunate condition."

"Well, that's why I am here."

"I trust the boy is well?"

"Yes. I've been getting to know him over the past few days, and he is a wonderful child. However, I fear he is wearing out his small body by dragging it about. His hands, the palms and knuckles, are red and raw, calloused heavily."

"Of course. Human hands were never intended to be walking appendages."

"His mother arrived two days ago. Her husband is deceased, and she is destitute. She has mentioned crutches that could be fitted for Enos, which would help him move around, but she does not have the means to acquire them. I'd like to purchase these crutches for him."

"Mr. Watson, do you have any idea of the cost of such things? They will need to be custom made for the boy. I will need to take measurements and to observe his locomotion, and then a carpenter will need to fashion them to my specifications. Have you brought money with you?"

"Mr. Dorfoy has not yet paid me. I hoped we could work out some sort of agreement. Perhaps I could run errands for you, or pay you in installments."

"I hardly need another errand boy. William easily handles all of that. I could provide the services on credit, and you can make regular payments. Perhaps Joseph will vouch for you."

"Wonderful!" I was concerned about Dorfoy's reaction to my plan, especially since I had concocted it during my workday. But, I did believe he had Enos's best interests in mind. After all, he was going to give Elizabeth all the proceeds from his display.

"I must meet my next appointment now," the doctor said. "I will pay a visit to the museum tomorrow to see the boy." He rose to leave his office.

"Thank you, thank you, doctor. Enos and his mother will be so appreciative!" I followed him out, giddy with what I had accomplished during my short visit.

# Chapter 10
## Mr. Dorfoy's Boot

*Elizabeth Stutsman*

M r. Dorfoy returned without Arthur, who had been sent out on a day's work. He approached the stage and snatched away the book that Enos had already started reading.

"I thought I told Mr. Watson to stay out of my office!"

Enos looked stunned. "But, Mr. Dorfoy, I was just going to thank you for leaving these books for me. I so love a good adventure!"

Mr. Dorfoy examined the book closely, turning it over in his hands to look at the spine, opening it up to see the inside cover.

"Cooper's *Last of the Mohicans?* This is not my book. Where did you get this?" he asked Enos.

"It was in the hall outside my door with the other books you left for me."

"I did not leave these books for you. Mr. Watson must have."

"No, Sir. Mr. Watson found them in the hall."

By then I had risen and walked over to them. "What is the trouble, Mr. Dorfoy?"

"Enos seems to have a mysterious benefactor. I did not

leave any books outside his door." He looked perplexed and flustered.

"Enos, why don't you continue reading?" I turned to Mr. Dorfoy. "Shall we take a turn about the room, sir?"

He took my arm, and we walked toward the windows. "Mr. Dorfoy, I don't know who gave my son the books, but please, it is his one pleasure. His only escape from this reality is his imagination. I think it best we not worry about the source of the books just now."

Mr. Dorfoy glanced back at the platform, where Enos had already forgotten about the conversation. He lay on his stomach, his head propped on his elbows, once again completely absorbed in the story.

"As you wish, Mrs. Stutsman. Nonetheless, I will ask Thomas and Ginny if they know anything about this."

Satisfied, I returned to my seat and resumed my needlework. Mr. Dorfoy immediately left to conduct his daily business, and the rest of the morning moved slowly. At times, the grand hall was as quiet as a church. The silence was occasionally punctuated by footsteps up the stairs and a cackle of voices. The visitors would gather around Enos and occasionally walk over to ask me questions, always a strange look of pity in their eyes. Then they would leave, walking back down the stairs and out onto the street, relieved they could turn their backs on such horror and return to the wonderful drudgery of their daily lives. In the end, this was Mr. Dorfoy's business—keeping people content with their terrible existence. Illness, stench, factory work, the struggle to pay the landlord, the cold seeping into their walls—all paled in comparison to what they saw at the museum. Thank God he's not my son, they must think. Thank God it's not me.

I had made Mr. Dorfoy's acquaintance the summer before Jacob passed. I was bustling about our storefront, tidying up just as we opened for the day. Jacob busied himself at his workbench, stretching leather around a shoe form. The heat had not dissipated the night before, so it was already close and uncomfortable inside. I pushed the door open to let in some air, and on our front stoop stood a well-dressed gentleman wearing a silk jacket and beaver top hat.

"Good day, madam," he said as he tipped his hat. "I am looking for someone to repair my boot heel. It lodged between cobblestones yesterday and nearly snapped off."

"Do come in, sir. We've just opened."

The man stepped inside. He minced with his left foot. "I hope you've not walked far with your heel like that," I said.

"No, madam. I arrived in the city just last evening. My shoe was damaged as I left my carriage in front of the hotel where I am staying a few doors down."

Jacob rose from his bench. "Let me see what we've got."

The gentleman first reached out his hand. "Joseph Dorfoy."

Jacob shook his hand. "Jacob Stutsman, and this is my wife, Elizabeth."

"Pleased to meet you, Mr. and Mrs. Stutsman." He sat

down to remove his shoe, exposing a clean, white stocking. Jacob took the shoe over to his workbench and turned it over to examine its sole.

"This is nothing serious, Mr. Dorfoy. Should take only a few minutes." He began pounding the heel with a small hammer.

Just then, Enos entered the room through the open door at the back of the storefront that led to the stairs to our living quarters. As he moved to the front of the shop, Mr. Dorfoy quickly stood up, shocked, wearing just one boot.

"Enos!" I said. "You should be studying your spelling." I moved to usher him back upstairs.

"It's alright, Mrs. Stutsman," said Mr. Dorfoy. "Please, bring him closer where I can see him."

I looked nervously at Jacob. He nodded to me, so I picked up Enos. He was only six years old at the time and very light. We were always anxious about the reactions Enos evoked in people. We were not ashamed of our child, but sometimes it was better for business if he stayed away from the shop.

"This is our son, Enos. Say hello to Mr. Dorfoy."

"Pleased to meet you, Mr. Dorfoy," said Enos, as he extended his hand toward the gentleman.

"Likewise, Master Stutsman," said Mr. Dorfoy. He smiled and shook my son's hand.

Jacob had already finished attaching the heel to Mr. Dorfoy's boot. He handed me a few coins for payment but then sat down again. I was puzzled as to why this very fine gentleman would want to stay in our shop any longer than necessary.

He began to speak. "I have come east from Cincinnati on business. I have already visited Baltimore to see Peale's museum and will next go to New York to see the American Museum and Peale's there."

"You see," he continued, "I am proprietor of the Western Museum in Cincinnati, the greatest institution of its kind in the West." I saw Jacob's eyes darken with realization.

Mr. Dorfoy stood up and handed Jacob his calling card. "I pay handsomely to those willing to show themselves to the public."

Jacob's face grew red. He narrowed his eyes. "Get out of my shop!" he yelled, throwing the card in Mr. Dorfoy's face.

"Mr. Stutsman, I assure you, it would be tasteful. Educational. It could help your family."

"Get out. Get out!" He pointed to the door.

"I'm very sorry, madam," he said as he tipped his hat to me and Enos. "My apologies to you, as well, Master Stutsman." He bowed and left our shop.

Jacob took Enos from me and, without a word, walked him back upstairs. I looked down and saw Mr. Dorfoy's calling card, face down, gleaming white on our worn wooden floor. I do not entirely know why, but I bent down and picked it up. Looking around the room, I saw a clay jar on the table in the corner. For whatever reason, I took the card over to the jar, placed it inside, and moved it to the highest shelf I could reach.

# Chapter 11
## A Terrible Time for Business

*Arthur Watson*

When I returned to the museum, a few visitors were poking around the collection in the entrance hall. They were so taken by the gigantic animal bones that they paid no attention to me. I breezed by them and hurried upstairs to Dorfoy's office.

"Mr. Dorfoy!" I called, knocking on the door. I waited a moment, then knocked again.

"Mr. D..." The door swung open.

"Did you discover something so utterly fascinating at Letton's that it couldn't wait until later?" His brow was furrowed. I obviously had interrupted something.

"Oh, yes, Letton's." I sank my hands in each pocket until I found the pamphlet and pulled it out, folded and wrinkled. I held it up in front of him.

He shook his head and sighed. "Just come in."

He sat in his leather chair, and on the desk before him, a large scrapbook lay open to two blank pages of heavy blue paper. I sat down across from him as I had the day of our first meeting.

"Well, let's hear your report." He didn't look up at me,

but remained focused on the scrapbook as I talked.

"I brought you this pamphlet. Letton's is showing a sea dog." I handed him the paper, and he motioned for me to set it down next to the scrapbook.

"Hmmm." He seemed only the least bit interested. In his left hand he held an engraving, and in his right, a brush. He turned the picture over and brushed some adhesive onto the back. His spectacles were perched on the end of his nose, and he peered down through them as he turned the illustration over again. As he smoothed it with his hands, I saw a horrifying picture of a child standing beneath the arching canopy of a tree, an extra torso and head growing from his chest. Depicted with stark black hatching on creamy paper, it could have been an elegant portrait if the child had been wearing clothes and not been so shockingly deformed.

It took me a second to regain my composure. "Yes, a sea dog. A truly delightful creature. It shuffled around on its flippers and did tricks when a man fed it fish."

"Is that all?"

"Well, yes. That was the newest exhibit. I have never seen anything like it." Sweat began to collect under my arms, and my face felt hot.

"I've seen at least three sea dogs at museums out East. The public loves them, but they are nothing new."

I wasn't sure what to say, so I blurted out the real reason I had rushed to his office. "When might I expect my first payment?" I gulped.

Dorfoy was silent for a moment as he turned the page in his scrapbook. "Do you owe a debt?" he asked calmly as he cut out another illustration.

"I owe Mrs. Gibson my room and board, but she has accommodated me so far and would be willing to wait a few more days."

"Why the rush, then?" He pressed a drawing of some insects onto a blue page.

"I may be making a substantial purchase within the next few days."

"What could you possibly need? If it's clothing, Ginny can make sure you get some new shirts and trousers. I provide your meals..."

"It is a gift, actually." I lifted my chin and smiled.

He put down the scissors and brush, pushed up his glasses, and looked directly at me. "Mr. Watson, you are hardly in a position to purchase gifts. You haven't a penny to your name."

"But I've been working for you three days now. I'd have thought that at least after one week I could expect some payment."

"Do you have any idea of the trouble this institution is in? Winter is a terrible time for business. Few people travel on the river in winter, and when the river freezes there is no one. I have performers to pay, not to mention Ginny and Thomas. I am providing food and lodging for the Stutsmans. We need oil for the lamps, wood to keep warm. What is it, a present for some woman?"

I was insulted he would think me so shallow. "No matter. Just tell me when I can expect my first payment." I tried my best to be stern, but my voice faltered.

Dorfoy thought for a moment. "Why don't I pay your

debt to Mrs. Gibson. There is an extra room you can stay in here. I usually reserve it for traveling performers who need to stay the night, but I don't expect I shall need it until summer."

That would at least buy me some time. I could perhaps strike a deal with Dr. Drake. "Fine." I didn't know what else to say. Dorfoy explained that he would arrange for Mrs. Gibson to receive payment by the end of the week and went right back to his scrapbook.

As I rose to leave, Dorfoy, without looking up from the scrapbook, said, "I almost forgot. There's a stack of letters over there that need to be delivered." He gestured toward a side table. "And, you'll need to go back to Letton's. A family of musical dwarves is performing this evening, and I require a full report." I picked up the letters and pulled the door closed behind me. I felt as though I had been kicked in the stomach.

That night, I explained the situation to Mrs. Gibson.

"I've so enjoyed your company in the mornings, Mr. Watson. I will be sad to see you go."

"Mr. Dorfoy will send a bank note by the end of the week."

"Have you met my daughter's husband yet?"

"Mr. Powers? No, ma'am. But I hope to soon. I've seen him around and am truly amazed by the lifelike qualities of his wax sculptures."

"You should speak with him very soon about your predicament with Mr. Dorfoy. He will certainly lend a sympathetic ear. He is very talented and kind as well, but

I fear he will leave us soon for better prospects."

"I will make a point of it, Mrs. Gibson."

"Very well. Tomorrow will be your last breakfast here?"

"Yes, ma'am."

"Well, I'll make it a special one, then."

"Good night, Mrs. Gibson. I am grateful for the kindness you have shown me."

She smiled and gave a quick curtsy. "Sleep well, Mr. Watson."

I lay in bed staring at the ceiling, my hands folded behind my head. Though I had known them only a few days, I missed being with Enos and Elizabeth tonight. I had left my own family almost ten days ago, but I did not miss them nearly as much as I did the boy and his mother. I thought about my parents and how I had left things back at the farm.

"We hope you'll have a change of heart, Arthur," my mother said, her eyes filling with tears. My father had barely spoken to me for the entire month since I had made my decision to go to Cincinnati.

"I hope Father will come to his senses. Harry needs this place. I've never loved it the way he does."

My brother Harold's passion was helping out around the farm, although he was not allowed to do the heavy work since his illness. I only did it because my father expected it of me. One day, the autumn before I made my announcement to the family, Harry and I walked to the creek. We sat on a log near the water as the crisp, clear air lifted the remaining leaves from the trees.

"You know Father wants you to take over the farm when he is gone," Harold said, throwing small pebbles into the creek.

"We won't have to think about that for a long time," I replied, watching the ripples spread to the water's edge.

"You are the eldest, so it only makes sense."

"And yet it makes no sense! You are only three years younger, and you love the land."

Harold looked out through the trees. The sun turned the field beyond the forest golden as it lowered in the sky.

"You appreciate the grazing cattle," I continued. "I've seen you alone with them, patting the sides of their huge heads as they grind grass in their mouths. You even slop the pigs with grace. I've only ever loved to play here, to run in the forest or to fish in the creek. I hate the work. I feel trapped by the rolling hills, lost in the rows and rows of corn, buried by piles of straw."

"You will never convince them I am strong enough."

"But you are! You were only a boy when you were sick. You are a young man now, and much stronger. Strong of body and of heart, which is more important. You will thrive here. You could raise a family and make a good home for them here. If I stay here much longer, I feel I should die."

As we sat together on that autumn day, I became resolved as to what I needed to do. My teachers had always told me I had a head for business, that I should go to the city where a smart young man could become a banker, merchant, or investor. Once I traded my straw hat for a top hat, my father would have to pass the farm to Harold. They would have no choice. In my leaving to pursue my dream, I would open the door for Harold's, too.

I had made it to Cincinnati and now must do anything it took to succeed for Harold's sake. The next morning, I packed what little I had into my bag—two shirts, one pair of trousers, a few letters, my leather journal, a razor. I had not brought much because I wanted to start fresh, and to be honest, I didn't own much to begin with. I carried the bag with me to the dining room where Mrs. Gibson had, as promised, prepared a hearty breakfast of bacon, coffee, and cornbread with berry preserves she had been saving for a special occasion. The smoky smell of frying bacon comforted my nerves. I wasn't completely sure about moving into the museum, but I knew it was my only option. As I swallowed the last, gritty mouthful of coffee, Mrs. Gibson sat down across from me.

"The best of luck to you, Mr. Watson," she said as she patted my arm with her plump hand. "And remember, if you need to, you can always come back here. There will always be a room for you."

I thanked her and reminded her that Dorfoy would send payment by week's end. She smiled at me sympathetically as I put on my coat, readying myself for the cold. I waved to her once more as I opened the door to leave.

The air outside was calm, and the western horizon hung heavy and dark. Only a little sunlight made its way through the clouds, sketching the buildings and streets in faint, bluish light. When I arrived at the museum, Dorfoy was in the entrance hall with Thomas.

"Mr. Watson! So glad you are here. I must go to Lawrenceburg today to see a collector. I'll need you to stay at the museum until this evening."

"But, Mr. Dorfoy, the weather may turn. There are clouds in the west. Couldn't this wait?"

"It is a very important collection of geological specimens. If I do not speak to him immediately, as he insisted in his letter, I may be unable to acquire it. The road to Lawrenceburg is clear and direct. If I leave now, I will make it by afternoon."

Thomas helped Dorfoy on with his coat.

"Mr. Watson, a visitor is due today for performances this evening and tomorrow evening," Dorfoy said as he put on his hat and gloves. "A phrenologist from Boston— Dr. Bell is his name. Please entertain him in my absence. I do hope to return before his eight o'clock show tonight."

"I shall take care of him and see to Enos and his mother, as well."

"But of course you will," Dorfoy replied, smirking. "Now, Thomas, come help me with the coach." And the two of them left me standing alone in the vestibule.

I headed upstairs to find Elizabeth and Enos already at their post.

"Good day, Mr. Watson," said Elizabeth. She was already stitching some fabric.

"Mr. Watson!" Enos's face lit up.

"Good morning to you both," I returned. "Mr. Dorfoy has taken leave for the day on important business. He has left me in charge." I was aware this may have been an overstatement.

"How wonderful," said Elizabeth, beaming. "You must tell us of your adventures yesterday."

I pulled a stool over to sit facing her. "Yes, but first, I'm pleased to report we will have some guests today."

"Oh?"

"A phrenologist from Boston will be here this afternoon. Mr. Dorfoy has hired him for two demonstrations."

"Fen-all-ah..." stammered Enos.

"Phrenologist, Enos. He is a doctor who explores the depths of the human mind. He studies a person's countenance and posture—all of his outward pecularities—to examine his character and virtues."

"It is my understanding that this is a very new discipline in America," said Elizabeth. "The Europeans have been doing it for years."

"Yes, Mr. Dorfoy must have worked very hard to bring Dr. Bell here."

"Will he study us?" asked Enos, looking concerned.

"I am not sure," I replied. "It is possible he will request volunteers for his demonstrations."

"Mr. Watson—you said guests, which implies more than one," said Elizabeth.

"Of course. Yesterday I paid Dr. Drake a visit. He will come to see Enos today."

"Enos? Whatever for? My son is quite healthy."

"Well," I thought for a second, "the doctor would like to check in with the boy, to see how he is adjusting to life here." I decided to leave the crutches as a surprise.

"How kind of him."

Just then, Elizabeth noticed the small bag I had carried in and set down next to my feet.

"What's this?" she asked.

"My satchel. Mr. Dorfoy has invited me to stay here in the museum."

"You will be our neighbor?" Enos asked.

"Well, I'm not sure where my room will be, but, yes, I will be in the building."

"That's strange," said Elizabeth. "Why would he do that?"

I didn't want to alarm her about the museum's financial crisis. "I think, Mrs. Stutsman, that Mr. Dorfoy felt I could do much more good here. I can spend more time working, you know, early and late in the day. I assure you, he has only the best interests of his business in mind."

"In any case," she said, "It will be nice to see you at breakfast." She smiled and returned to her needlework.

Because I felt responsible for the workings of the museum, I felt I should make the rounds, just to see that all was well. I also needed to alert Ginny and Thomas to Dr. Drake's expected visit. "I will return shortly, Mrs. Stutsman," I said. I picked up my bag and took my leave.

I first toured the second floor, poking my head into each room. The cosmorama was quiet, as was the gallery of minerals and the room of bird specimens. Little light came in through the windows on this cloudy day, so I searched for Ginny to ask her to light the lamps. I found her downstairs, dusting the fossils in the entrance hall.

"Good day, Ginny."

"Good morning, Mr. Watson. Mr. Dorfoy is out for the day."

"Yes, I know. He asked me to mind things while he is away."

"Mein Gott! I almost forgot," she said, eyeing my bag. "Let me show you to your room." She dropped her duster and began waddling toward a long hall I had not yet been down.

We passed several doors. Behind one, I heard tapping. "What's in there?" I asked.

"That's Mr. Powers' workshop."

How convenient, I thought. I will need to pay him a visit today.

Ginny stopped at a door at the end of the hall. "This is it, Mr. Watson," she said as she fiddled with the key. "It's nothin' fancy, but you'll be comfortable here." She pushed the door open. A high window let in a bit of light, just enough to reveal a nondescript bed with two woolen blankets folded at its end, a table with a wash basin in the corner, a wooden chair next to the door, and a small chest of drawers beneath the window. The room was cold and smelled dusty, as if it had not been used for a long while.

"I guess this is home," I said, placing my bag inside. I wouldn't be spending much time there, anyway, except to sleep.

"I will bring you a lamp and a bedwarmer, and Thomas will bring you some wood for the stove."

"Thank you, Ginny. Oh, and we are expecting a guest today."

"Yes, Dr. Bell. Mr. Dorfoy already informed me."

"There will be another. Dr. Drake will be by today as well. And, would you mind lighting the lamps upstairs? It's a dark day, and it's difficult to see the exhibits."

"Certainly, Mr. Watson. But, there won't be many visitors today. Thomas says a storm is brewin'."

"A storm? But, Mr. Dorfoy is out there."

"Thomas tried to tell him, but Mr. Dorfoy does as Mr. Dorfoy wants. There's no stopping him when he sets his mind to something."

I pushed past Ginny and ran down the hall. I searched everywhere for Thomas, and when I couldn't find him, I ran to the entrance hall and out onto the street. It was immediately evident that a storm was heading toward the city. The clouds hung low in the sky, and sleet had already begun to fall. I looked in the direction of the public landing. People hauled firewood and checked their shutters. Shop owners hung signs on their doors. A man walked by and greeted me with an abrupt, "Storm's coming today."

Thomas came from around the corner with a bundle of wood on his shoulder. "Mr. Watson—what are you doin' out here?"

"Thomas! We have to fetch Mr. Dorfoy."

"Agh, Mr. Watson. No worries. Mr. Dorfoy will reach Lawrenceburg by afternoon, well before things turn ugly. He's a smart man. He'll stay the night if he must. Besides, his best driver is with him. If he has a lick of sense, he won't try to come back tonight."

I was a bit relieved by Thomas' logic. I certainly did not want to be caught in a blizzard alone on a horse. We were taught never to venture out in a winter storm in Pennsylvania, as one could easily lose his way. Landmarks disappear in a white out, and once your clothes were wet from snow, sleet, or rain, you could die from exposure in hours. Of course, these thoughts only added to my concern about Dorfoy.

"I trust you are right, Thomas," I said as I opened the door for him.

# Chapter 12
## The Phrenologist

*Arthur Watson*

I had begun to wonder if Dr. Drake would still pay us a visit, considering the weather. However, his office and home were within a short walk, and by afternoon he arrived. As usual, Enos had whiled away the morning with his nose in a book. Elizabeth continued her needlework, of which there seemed no shortage, and I chatted with her on occasion. The three of us were in the grand hall when the doctor emerged from the staircase, removing his hat to reveal his tousled hair. His shoulders were wet, and he left a trail of slush behind him as he walked over to greet us.

"I am grateful to you for venturing out in this terrible weather," I said as I shook his hand.

"It is not so bad, really. However, the sleet has frozen on the ground, and I have already made a few calls to those who have slipped and injured themselves. One gentleman, poor fool, fell and hit his head on his doorstep. His dear wife found him there unconscious. You can imagine the hysterics!"

"How awful!" said Elizabeth, her fingers playing with her lace collar. "I hope he is well?"

"Yes, quite. Nothing a bit of smelling salts couldn't cure, for both him and his wife," Dr. Drake said, his eyes gleaming.

"Enos, please come over and say hello to Dr. Drake."

"But, Mama, I am almost finished with this poem!"

"Enos..."

"Certainly, Mama."

Enos put down his book and made his way down the steps and over to us. He reached up to Dr. Drake with his hand. "Pleased to see you, Dr. Drake."

"Likewise, Enos," the doctor replied, taking the boy's hand in his and crouching down to speak to him.

"So, you like poetry?"

"Only Poe's."

"Mmm. Tales of suspense. You have good taste."

"Thank you, doctor."

"Well, you seem to be getting along well here. Your friend Mr. Watson came to see me yesterday and wanted me to pay you a visit."

"I am not sick," Enos replied, looking at me.

"Of course not," Dr. Drake said. "But he was hoping to help you in some way."

Elizabeth turned toward me. "What does he speak of, Mr. Watson?"

"I see you have not told her or the boy."

"I wanted to surprise them," I said, pleased with myself.

"Surprise us with what?" asked Elizabeth, her voice quivering.

"I have come to measure Enos for some crutches."

"Crutches! Mama, we have wanted those for so long!"

Elizabeth just stood there. She glanced from Enos to the doctor and then to me. Looking back at the boy, she said gently, "But, Enos, you know we cannot afford them."

"That is why I went to see Dr. Drake," I announced.

Now something rose inside Elizabeth. Her chest began rising and falling faster, and her eyes narrowed. "How dare you," she said, under her breath. "How dare you, Mr. Watson."

"But, I don't understand."

"You raise my son's hopes like this? Only to have them dashed again?" Her face reddened. "We will not take charity. You are not his father. You are not even old enough to be his father! You truly have no idea." She turned to Enos. "Go. Get your book."

"But, Mama…"

"Go!"

Enos sighed and looked down at the floor. The doctor tried to explain to Elizabeth as Enos moved toward the stage.

"Do you see, Mrs. Stutsman, the strain he puts on his arms and hands?" He gestured toward the boy. "He cannot go on like this forever. His body will suffer irreparable damage."

When Enos returned, she picked him up. "We are done here for today." Tears welled in her eyes as she turned toward the stairs. The boy looked back at us over her shoulder as they left the grand hall.

"I apologize, doctor," I said. "I do not understand Mrs.

Stutsman's reaction. She has said herself the boy needs the crutches."

"Mr. Watson, do you not understand pride? You should have spoken to her before coming to see me."

"I will go to her now and convince her."

He put his hand on my shoulder. "My dear boy, sometimes is it best to leave a woman be."

"But..."

"Give her some time. I trust she will come to her senses."

"Thank you for taking the time to come here. I understand if you must leave now, as I am sure you have other calls to make."

"I'd rather stay out of the dreadful cold. My assistant knows where to find me if necessary. Now, is there somewhere in this place we can have a drink?"

We descended the stairs and at the end of the first floor corridor saw Ginny still tidying up. She had just moved a small case of Indian cooking implements away from the wall to clean behind it when she saw us.

"Sir! Mr. Watson!" she called, scurrying toward us. "Dr. Bell has arrived. I told him he would find you upstairs, but he wanted to look around a bit first."

"Thank you, Ginny" I replied.

The doctor turned toward me. "Is it not Dr. Damien Bell? The phrenologist?"

"Yes, it is."

"How serendipitous! I read in the gazette that he was to perform demonstrations here. I had hoped to meet him to discuss his discipline."

"Ginny—please bring us some whiskey to the dining room."

"Certainly, Mr. Watson."

Dr. Drake and I peeked into each room looking for the new guest. We finally found him in the gallery with the snake.

"Good day, Dr. Bell," I said.

"Good day," he said, without looking at me. "I am completely enthralled by this creature!"

"It is an anaconda from South America," I responded.

He turned toward us. "Please, accept my apologies for such an inattentive greeting." He looked much younger than I had expected for a doctor. His golden blond hair fell over his brow, setting off clear, blue eyes and clean-shaven, chiseled features still ruddy from the winter air.

"Apologies accepted. I am Mr. Watson, and this is Dr. Drake."

"Dr. Daniel Drake? Your reputation precedes you."

"As does yours, Dr. Bell," Dr. Drake replied dryly.

The two men shook hands. "Do you intend to mount a demonstration this evening?" Dr. Drake asked.

"I had intended. That is, until this blasted weather set in. It would be a wonder if anyone came. Now, where is Mr. Dorfoy?"

"I am sorry to report, Dr. Bell, that Mr. Dorfoy is indisposed. He left town for business this morning and had hoped to return before your demonstration. However, as you have already noted, the weather will surely keep him for the night."

"How disappointing. I had wanted to discuss my program with him and, of course, to become better acquainted. Mr. Dorfoy has built a enthralling institution here."

"You shall have time when he returns," I replied.

"Well, I believe we will have some fascinating conversation," offered Dr. Drake. "Please join us for a drink."

The three of us proceeded down the corridor, the two doctors ahead of me, already excitedly discussing matters of science as I followed behind. When we arrived at the dining room, Ginny had already left us three glasses and a bottle. I had not swallowed a drop of whiskey since Elizabeth's tirade on the day she arrived, but I could certainly use some now. We sat down, the doctors across from each other, and myself next to Dr. Drake. I poured us each a glass.

"Are you a follower of Spurzheim?" Dr. Drake asked.

"I began my study with François Gall's writings but soon recognized Spurzheim's genius. I had the pleasure of meeting him in Boston two years ago during his lecture tour. His manner was far less pompous than Dr. Caldwell's, who as you know is the foremost American scholar on the subject."

"Dr. Spurzheim's passing was a terrible tragedy, but you do realize his theories have little basis in science," said Dr. Drake.

"Their foundations are in observation," said Dr. Bell.

"They are little more than performance," retorted Dr. Drake.

I tried to follow their conversation as best I could, and joined in, hoping to soften the argument that began to rear its head. "I do remember reading about Spurzheim. Am I correct in my recollection that he lectured in New York, then Boston, and had intended a much wider tour but fell ill and died?"

"That is correct," said Dr. Bell. "He had just begun to open the minds of the public, at least those intelligent enough to grasp his theories, to their moral and intellectual powers. It is fortunate, however, that others like myself have devoted their lives to cultivating his ideas. Let us have a toast to Spurzheim," he said, lifting his glass.

"To science," replied Dr. Bell, emptying his glass. I drank as well, and the liquid burned as it went down. I filled our glasses again.

The doctors continued their discussion. As they tossed around words I didn't understand, my thoughts drifted elsewhere, to Elizabeth's face, contorted in anger and sadness as she left the room with Enos.

My attention returned as Dr. Drake said, "Although our opinions differ, Dr. Bell, you must see the rest of the collection."

"Yes, indeed. We can agree to disagree. There is certainly no harm in a friendly debate," said Dr. Bell. "In Mr. Dorfoy's absence, I would be honored to receive a personal tour from the founder of the museum. Mr. Watson, will you join us?"

"I have some business to attend to," I replied, not sure exactly what I meant. "But I hope to see you later. You

are both invited to stay for our evening meal. Ginny is a
wonderful cook."

"Thank you, Mr. Watson, but my wife will be
expecting me."

"Very well. Please say good-bye before you go."

"I will, of course, accept your invitation," said Dr. Bell.

The two men walked out of the room, leaving me
alone. I sighed and put my head down on the worn,
wooden tabletop, and my hand bumped the cool, glass
bottle. I lifted my head and poured myself another glass
of whiskey. It went down more smoothly than the last,
so I poured another. And another.

# Chapter 13
## The Faculties of the Mind

*Elizabeth Stutsman*

Enos and I spent the entire afternoon in my room. He lay on the bed, wrapped in the quilt I had sent with him, reading aloud to me while I finished some needlepoint. Ginny had given me some linen handkerchiefs to decorate, and I was embellishing them with a floral border and wreaths of entwined leaves in each corner. The complicated design kept my mind and hands busy, making the dark hours of this stormy day pass quickly. I wanted to speak to no one save my son. I still could not believe Arthur's audacity, but was equally embarrassed by my outburst. It was not proper behavior for a lady.

Evening came before we knew it. Enos was hungry and begged to go to supper, so I steeled myself to join the others. I smoothed my hair, pinched my cheeks, and took a deep breath, telling myself it would be over in just an hour. We would then all go to bed and have forgotten about everything by morning.

The museum was the quietest it had been since I arrived. On our way to the dining room, I peered out a window in the corridor. Not a soul moved on the street.

The sleet had changed to snow, and the wind whipped it into high drifts along the buildings. I lifted Enos so he could see, too. He looked at me with furrowed eyebrows.

"Don't fret about Mr. Dorfoy," I told him. "He is safe in Indiana and will return in the morning when the weather has cleared." His face calmed, and I prayed that what I had said was indeed true.

We arrived at the dining room to find Thomas seated at the table with a young gentleman. They both stood up.

"Hello, Mrs. Stutsman. This here's Dr. Bell."

The gentleman stepped forward and took my hand. I curtsied and looked back up at him. "Pleased to make your acquaintance, doctor." He gazed into my eyes, which made me nervous. "Dr. Bell, this is my son, Enos."

"Ah, yes. Enos—I've heard much about you already."

"From Mr. Watson?" Enos asked eagerly.

"Actually, from Dr. Drake. He holds both you and your mother in high esteem." He looked back at me and smiled.

I found this strange, since Dr. Drake had spoken to us only briefly on two occasions, the second of which included my emotional outburst that afternoon.

"Dr. Drake sends his apologies that he could not join us. He returned home to dine with his family."

"Is Mr. Watson coming?" asked Enos.

"I expect he will join us. He had business to attend to, so I spent the past few hours with Dr. Drake, who gave me the most splendid tour of the museum."

"Did you see the Infernal Regions?" Enos asked.

"Enos, I am sure Dr. Bell is concerned mainly with the

scientific collections here," I said, "and I surely think the Regions will be closed this evening in Mr. Dorfoy's absence."

"Actually," said the doctor, "I have heard much about the Regions, but I don't believe there will be time for me to see it, as I will perform demonstrations both tonight and tomorrow evening. However, I plan to return to Cincinnati periodically in the future and will certainly take in the exhibition then."

We moved to the table to take our seats. Thomas and Enos sat on one side of the table, and Dr. Bell helped me into my chair first, then sat down next to me.

"So, what kind of doctor are you again?" asked Enos.

"Enos—be polite!" I scolded.

"That's perfectly fine, Mrs. Stutsman. Enos, I practice phrenology."

"What is that, exactly?" asked Thomas.

"Honestly," I said, "Must we interrogate the doctor?"

"Really, it's all right. I enjoy explaining my discipline, as it is relatively new to America, especially to those without a formal education."

I saw Thomas' eyes narrow, but he remained curious.

"Thomas, stay seated." Dr. Bell walked around the table to him. "It is far easier if I demonstrate on a live subject."

"I don't much like doctors touchin' me," said Thomas.

"I assure you," Dr. Bell chuckled, "this will not hurt a bit."

Enos watched intently.

"Ginny!" I called. "You must come here this moment.

Dr. Bell is going to demonstrate on Thomas!" Thomas grumbled.

"You see," began Dr. Bell, "The mind itself is composed of many different organs, each carrying the propensities, sentiments, and faculties that make up our intellect and character." He placed his hands on Thomas's head.

"What the..." said Thomas.

"It's perfectly safe, Thomas."

Dr. Bell began moving his fingers around Thomas' head, tousling his hair. Thomas scowled, and his cheeks flushed.

"The form of the head, its bumps and crevices, corresponds with the form of the brain. It represents the development of the organs of the brain, the faculties of the mind."

"What does Thomas's head say?" asked Enos.

"Hmm... well, this bump near the back center of Thomas's skull indicates his firmness. The one behind this ear suggests combativeness."

"Nothin' but hocus-pocus," mumbled Thomas.

"This little valley here," probed Dr. Bell, "means your language abilities are a bit underdeveloped."

"That's enough!" said Thomas.

"Wait... this raised area above your right temple suggests your wit is above average."

"Hmm," huffed Thomas.

"And this area on the side of the top of your cranium points to your conscientiousness."

Everyone in the room clapped, and Dr. Bell gave a

quick bow.

"Not a bad science, this is," said Thomas, smiling.

"Now do Mama!" said Enos.

"Oh, heaven's no!" I said.

"Why not, Mrs. Stutsman?" Ginny and Thomas goaded me on.

"I simply couldn't. I…"

Before I knew it, Dr. Bell was behind me, his hands on my head. Enos laughed. What else could I do but let him perform his little demonstration? He pulled at the two pins that held my chignon, and I felt my hair cascade down my back.

"Now, let's see. Ah! Here we are." His fingers moved around my skull, sending shivers down my neck. "The middle of your forehead is slightly elevated, indicating individuality."

"That is you, Mama," exclaimed Enos.

I felt the warmth of Dr. Bell's hands through my hair. "And these regions on both the top left and right of the skull show you are full of hope. This area here," he felt the top of my head toward the back, "sinks in slightly, indicating a deficiency in self-esteem."

I grew nervous. "Perhaps we should stop."

"Nonsense—it is nothing to be ashamed of. Very common in women." I shifted in my chair. His hands were now on both sides of my head, his thumbs wrapped around the back of my neck. "These pronounced areas a few inches back from your temples represent a propensity for secretiveness."

Ginny giggled uncontrollably. Just as I grabbed at his

hands to make him stop, the door flew open.

"Mr. Watson!" said Enos. "Dr. Bell is demonstrating on Mama!"

Arthur stood in the doorway as if frozen. I froze, too, with my palms on top of Dr. Bell's hands.

"He's just finished," I said, pulling the doctors' hands from my head and twisting my hair, pinning it quickly into a loose knot at the nape of my neck.

"Good evening, Mr. Watson," said Dr. Bell. "I am sorry you could not join Dr. Drake and me this afternoon."

Arthur moved toward the table and took a seat next to Thomas. "What, to listen to the two of you go on about medicine? What a bore."

I had not yet heard Arthur speak this way. "Mr. Watson, Dr. Bell is Mr. Dorfoy's guest. We should make him feel welcome."

Ginny left the room and returned with a platter of pork. Arthur said nothing but grabbed a few pieces of meat and dropped them on his plate.

"Oh, I'm sorry. Our guest should have first choice." He picked up the pork with his hands and put it back on the platter.

"Mr. Watson!" I said, horrified.

"What did you do all afternoon, Mr. Watson?" Dr. Bell spoke. "Dr. Drake and I last saw you with a bottle of whiskey."

All eyes shot toward Arthur. "I took care of some business," he slurred.

I glared at him. Suddenly it was obvious—he was

utterly intoxicated.

He continued. "And what did you do all day, Dr. Bell? Run your fingers through Mrs. Stutsman's hair?"

"Mr. Watson! Watch your tongue. There is a lady present and a child," said Dr. Bell.

I stood up. "Ginny, please prepare a tray. Enos and I will dine in my room this evening." I picked up Enos and made my way to the door.

"It was lovely meeting you, Dr. Bell."

He rose and walked over. "Likewise, Madam, and your son as well. May I see you to your room?"

"Yes, I believe you may."

Arthur's eyes were riveted to me. I quickly turned, and Dr. Bell followed me out of the room.

"Good night, Mr. Watson," called Enos.

# Chapter 14
## The Devil's Drink

*Arthur Watson*

I woke up to the smell of coffee, my back cramped and my head throbbing. Thomas pushed a steaming mug over to me. "Drink this," he said.

"Where am I?" I asked, slowly realizing that I was still in the dining room.

"You went out cold," said Thomas. "Slumped clean over on the table, right after Mrs. Stutsman stormed outa here."

I thought hard, blinking a few times to clear my blurry eyes. "How long have I been here?"

"About a half-hour. C'mon. Drink it."

I lifted the coffee to my lips, but the minute the scent hit my nostrils, a wave of nausea passed through me. I quickly set it back down again.

"Well, son, you sure made a mess of things."

I thought again, and glimpses of memory rose in my mind. I saw Dr. Bell touching Elizabeth's head, her hair flowing over her shoulders, and Enos laughing. I saw Elizabeth's face shrouded with anger as she and Dr. Bell walked out the door.

"What have I done, Thomas?" I stood up, but the

117

room spun, sending me back into my seat.

"Relax, Mr. Watson. Just a bit of the devil's drink," Thomas chuckled.

"She will never forgive me. She will never let me speak to Enos again." My head sank onto the table.

"Look here. That kinda attitude ain't gonna solve nothin'. You just give it time and then say you're sorry." He patted me on the shoulder. "Women are stubborn, but they always come around. Especially for a nice young man like yourself."

"I'm going to bed." I rose, more slowly this time, and managed to drag myself toward the door.

"Not a bad idea," said Thomas. "I'll help you to your room."

I tried to sleep, but each time I closed my eyes, the bed felt as though it were spiraling down a deep chasm. I stared up in the darkness. I knew how Elizabeth felt about whiskey, but each swallow I took had made me feel stronger, more confident. I remembered the first time I tasted whiskey, when I was just about ten, cleaning stalls in the barn. I moved some boards leaning against the wall and found a bottle that one of our farmhands must have hidden. I put the boards back, walked over to the doors, and looked around outside. The men were all busy in the fields, so I closed the doors and retrieved the bottle. I climbed into the hayloft, where slivers of light streamed in between the slats in the roof. I held up the bottle to the light, swishing the amber liquid inside, and opened it to sniff its contents—sweet and pungent, a bit spicy. I put the bottle to my lips and tipped it back. The minute the spirits hit my tongue I gagged but swallowed anyway. It burned like fire going down and hit my stomach like a brick. I coughed and spit to rid my mouth of the taste and corked the bottle again.

I lay there in the straw for a while, holding up the bottle, shaking it, and watching the golden fluid slosh back and forth inside the glass. I decided to give it one more try, and that time I could taste its sweetness. The burning now felt more like a soothing line of warmth reaching from my throat, down my chest, and into my stomach. I took one more swig before corking the bottle and making my way down the ladder. My feet felt light, as if they floated above each rung, and my hands tingled. When I reached the ground, I looked around the barn, searching for the bottle's hiding spot. I blinked hard to focus my eyes and saw the boards not far from me. I walked toward them but discovered I could not walk a straight line. I took a deep breath and tried again. After I replaced the bottle behind the boards, I slumped to the floor and began to giggle. I could not stop laughing, even as my father opened the barn doors. Bright sunlight shot through the barn, nearly blinding me. Still giggling, I covered my eyes with my forearm.

I finally fell asleep with that feeling of warm sunlight hitting my face, the prickling of straw against my legs, and my father's strong grasp around my upper arm, lifting me up off the ground.

# Chapter 15
## A Most Amiable Gentleman

*Elizabeth Stutsman*

"I am very sorry you were upset by Mr. Watson's irresponsible behavior," said Dr. Bell as he ushered me down the hall, holding a small lamp to light our way. Darkness filled the corridors, since Ginny thought it best to conserve oil tonight in the absence of patrons at the museum.

"What was wrong with him, Mama?" Enos asked.

I searched for an answer that he would understand when Dr. Bell said, "Mr. Watson wasn't feeling well this evening. He just needed some sleep."

"Thank you," I told him. "I was not sure how to explain."

We approached Enos's room. "Enos, why don't you go inside and clean up. Ginny will be by soon with our supper trays."

"But, Mama, I did that already..."

"Come, Enos, at least straighten your hair. I'll be back for you shortly when the food arrives." I opened his door, and he went inside.

"I am not quite sure what came over Mr. Watson. He seemed such a gentleman these past days," I said.

"How long have you known him?"

"Only three days, since my arrival here."

"Sometimes one's true character reveals itself over time. How I would love to examine him, to unlock the secrets of his mind."

"He has disappointed me to a great degree. I expressed my belief in temperance the day we met, and still he has displayed this most base disrespect toward me. Certainly, an enlightened man such as yourself is aware of the moral degradation caused by the demon liquor."

Dr. Bell cleared his throat. "Of course, Mrs. Stutsman. Wicked stuff, that whiskey." He looked down at the floor when he said this, for the subject must have made him uncomfortable.

"Well, enough about Mr. Watson. I, too, must apologize for my behavior. I am sorry I acted as such a juvenile, Dr. Bell."

"No apology necessary. My subjects are often shocked and surprised by what my examinations unveil. It is I who should apologize. I fear I may have acted too boldly for our first meeting."

I hoped he would not see my face blush in the dim light. "Perhaps we can start again tomorrow. I understand you will stay on for a demonstration in the evening?"

"As you know, I had planned one for tonight, but it would be difficult with no audience. The weather should clear overnight, and Mr. Dorfoy will have returned. He has scheduled another demonstration at seven o'clock tomorrow evening. I do hope you will be there."

"Most certainly. What shall you do for the earlier parts of the day?"

"I have some important clients to visit early in the morning, and I have promised Dr. Drake I would pay calls to a few of his patients in the afternoon. But I do plan to dine here at the museum in the evening with Mr. Dorfoy. I could arrange for you and Enos to join us."

"Oh, we do not want to be any trouble." The suggestion made me nervous—Mr. Dorfoy did not eat in the dining room with the rest of the staff. And, besides, Enos only received a short meal break during his work hours, unless we dined very late as we did this evening.

"Nonsense. I will call for you after my demonstration." He nodded his head slowly toward me. "Now, I bid you goodnight, Mrs. Stutsman."

"Goodnight, Dr. Bell."

Ginny passed him as he walked down the hall.

"Here is your tray, Ma'am."

"Thank you, Ginny. Please put it in Enos's room. We will eat there tonight."

I grew very tired after our supper. "Time for bed, Enos."

"I'd like to read for a while, Mama."

"That's fine, but remember to put out your light before falling asleep."

"I will. Good night, Mama." I leaned down, and he planted a kiss on my cheek.

"Good night, son." I kissed his forehead.

Back in my room, I lit a candle, poured water into the

bowl in the corner, and splashed some on my face and neck. The cold liquid awakened my senses, promising to stave off sleep for a while. I loosened my stays and lifted my dress over my head, feeling the release from those heavy, tight layers. I then removed my petticoats and climbed into bed in my cotton shift.

I thought back on the day and wondered if every day at the museum felt as though it were filled with enough activity for an entire month. Mr. Dorfoy's absence during the storm, Dr. Drake's visit, Dr. Bell's arrival, Arthur's offer of crutches for Enos, and later his rudeness. I tried to clear my mind, but it was all too much. I wondered if someone would tell Mr. Dorfoy of Arthur's terrible behavior and if that person should be me. After all, he was to act as Mr. Dorfoy's ambassador, yet he insulted an important guest. And yet, I felt there was a reason to hold my tongue. Arthur hurt me greatly with his words, but I still perceived something pure in his character— Enos liked him very much. My son was not a typical child and perhaps because of his appearance he had developed the rare skill of sensing someone's sincerity almost immediately. I resolved to hold Arthur at arm's length. I would not apologize but decided to give him one more chance.

Then there was Dr. Bell, a most amiable gentleman. I truly enjoyed his company, but I felt strangely violated, as if his hands had reached into my very soul and pulled out things that have never been exposed to light and air. I did not fully grasp his science, but I could not deny its accuracy. I remembered drawing in my breath as his fingertips traced my scalp. I went over his words again and again in my mind. Individuality—of course I had always been a headstrong girl, which had gotten me into trouble more than once. Self-esteem—I try to be confident, especially for Enos, but inside I wonder if I have made the right choices for my son. Hope—does any mother lack this faculty? Do we not all want the best for our children? But the most troubling was his last revelation—secretiveness. Weren't there simply some things that should never be told?

# Chapter 16
## Mr. Powers' Studio

*Arthur Watson*

Something woke me abruptly. Not a noise or a presence so much as a thought I could not pin down. It propelled me into a series of worries. I would most certainly lose my job because of my behavior last night. I would never be able to speak to Enos again, and even worse, Elizabeth must hate me. I'd have nowhere to live, cast out onto the cold street. Of course, I could go back to Mrs. Gibson's, but I could not face her kindness without the ability to compensate her for her trouble. I sat up, fighting the urge to lie back down again. My head felt large and heavy, my tongue dry as a lump of cotton. How could I face anyone? Mr. Dorfoy would send me away as an impolite, incompetent, oaf, and who would hire someone with that sort of reputation? Dr. Bell must think me an imbecile. Elizabeth likely believes me an intemperate drunkard. Only one possibility lightened my heart—it was early, and Enos would be somewhere in the museum on his daily adventure.

I dressed quickly and looked out my tiny window. The sun had already risen, and it appeared the day would be clear. Mr. Dorfoy would likely return by afternoon, which meant I had to get to work immediately. I headed out into the hall and walked toward the entrance to the museum. The first door I passed was Mr. Powers' studio, and I heard tapping and grinding from inside. I continued on but was drawn back by another sound. It was a child's lilting voice coming from the studio. The door was ajar, so I stood there listening quietly for a moment.

"Show me how you make the hands look so real!" said Enos.

"Great care must be taken with the wax," replied the artist. "First, I build it up, then I cut it away carefully. As I get closer to finishing, I use these tiny tools. But I won't work on details until full daylight."

I looked in and saw a row of high windows through which sunlight was just beginning to enter. Powers worked near a candle, and I could see him heating a metal tool in its flame.

"Pardon me," I called.

"Who's there?" the artist asked.

"I am Mr. Watson, Mr. Dorfoy's assistant."

"Mr. Watson!" called Enos. "Good morning! I hope you're feeling better today. Come in, and see what Mr. Powers is making."

"Yes, please, come in," said Powers. He rose to greet me, wearing a long apron covered with drips of melted wax and streaks of paint.

"I'm delighted to finally meet you," I said, extending my hand. "I have heard much about you and have admired your work since I arrived."

"Yes, Enos told me of your visit to the Infernal Regions. I've had such great fun with it." Powers' deep, brown eyes sparkled when he spoke.

"It was indeed invigorating. Both frightening and entertaining."

"I'll let you in on a little secret," Powers said quietly, leaning in close. "Perhaps you saw a robed man skulking about in the exhibit?"

"Oh, yes," I replied.

"Well," he held his hand up to his nose, wrenching his fingers into a claw-like gesture. "Imagine the pincer from a lobster, right about here!"

I looked carefully at his face and then suddenly recognized him as the devilish, hooded being who wove in and out between members of the audience. "How uncanny! I never would have guessed."

"I have endeavored to make the movement of the wax automata to be very lifelike, but there is still no substitute for a living, breathing being who can interact with the audience. It is quite entertaining for me, as well!"

We walked into his studio where Enos sat on a tall stool. Two disembodied wax hands lay on the worktable, and an armless, headless wax figure stood nearby.

"He is making hands for… what is it called again?" asked Enos.

"An exquisite," replied the sculptor. "A fancy word for a well-bred gentleman. People love to see the latest fashions from Europe displayed on a lifelike model. I've already completed his companion," and he gestured over to the corner, where a lovely female figure with a tiny waist stood wearing an elegant, yellow evening gown and hat embellished with a plume of white feathers.

"She looks positively alive!" I said.

"That is the point," he chuckled.

"Mr. Dorfoy showed me your cannibal king," I said. "Very impressive."

"I'd rather not discuss that unfortunate incident," said Powers. "Sometimes Dorfoy goes too far."

The three of us were quiet for a few minutes while Enos and I watched Powers' hands deftly working, forming the wax fingers into what seemed to be a gesture of greeting. Then I got up the courage to ask. "Enos, how is your mother this morning?"

"She is well, Mr. Watson. She hummed a little tune at breakfast and said something about Dr. Bell inviting us to dine with him."

I swallowed. "About my... impudence last night, Enos. I hope you will forgive me."

"It's all right. Dr. Bell said you were ill. I'm glad to see you are better today."

"Yes, feeling much better. Now, shouldn't you be off to breakfast? Your mother will worry if you are late." I helped Enos off the stool.

"Mama always worries about me."

"Enos," said Powers. "I trust you are enjoying the books I've left for you?"

"Very much, sir. Today it is Irving's *Sketchbook*."

"Ah, yes. One of my favorites. You shall love 'Rip van Winkle.'"

"I am anticipating 'The Legend of Sleepy Hollow' even more," said Enos as he left the workshop.

"So you were the one?" I asked Powers.

"Yes, of course," replied the artist. "A boy should constantly exercise his imagination."

"I could not agree more. Enos's phenomenal imagination and intelligence could benefit from formal education, as well. His display here will be worthwhile if it brings enough money to help his mother in that regard."

"May I be frank with you, Mr. Watson?"

"Certainly."

"Mrs. Stutsman should be wary of Dorfoy's promises."

"How so?"

"Mr. Dorfoy is a good man. I impressed him with my mechanical work on an organ I helped build for the museum when he became its proprietor. He risked hiring me permanently some six years ago when I had barely demonstrated my sculpting abilities, and I have been able to hone my skills ever since. The situation has brought much public attention to my work."

"So, why the distrust?"

"I'll cut to the chase, Mr. Watson. Dorfoy, well intentioned as he is, has not always compensated me fairly. He has at times gone months without paying me, and I have a wife and an infant son to feed. Fortunately, my wife's family has been very generous."

"So that is what Mrs. Gibson meant."

"You know my mother-in-law?"

"Yes, I should have mentioned it right away. I stayed

at her boarding house when I arrived here. She was very kind to me, but I was able to pay her very little, that is, until Dorfoy agreed to fulfill my debt to her in exchange for my moving into a room at the museum."

"Then you must take care as well, Mr. Watson."

I sighed and thought for a moment. "Mrs. Gibson said she feared you may leave the city soon?"

"My tenure at the museum has finally brought me some portrait work. I just received my first commission in marble—a bust of one of the region's great reverends. Nicholas Longworth, my most gracious patron, has also expressed his desire to have me model his likeness."

"That is wonderful news. But with so much new business here, why leave?"

"The best prospects in America for any portrait sculptor are in Washington, Mr. Watson. I must go where there are many important men to immortalize. Through my newly made connections with Mr. Longworth, I hope to depart later this year."

"Surely Mr. Dorfoy will be sorry to see you go. How will he carry on the museum without you?"

"Such an enterprising man will certainly find a way."

I could see Powers was very busy. He carved the wax slowly and carefully now, incising lines in the knuckles and the curved edges around the fingernails.

"It was a pleasure to finally meet you, Mr. Powers. I shall leave you to concentrate on your work now."

"The pleasure was mine, Mr. Watson. Please do stop in again soon. I understand you are right down the hall."

"Yes, I am, and indeed I shall."

I turned to walk out of Powers' workshop, returning in my mind to what he had said about Dorfoy. I resolved to warn Elizabeth immediately and headed directly upstairs to the grand hall.

# Chapter 17
## The Cosmorama

*Arthur Watson*

The hall was quiet as always during the morning. Elizabeth sat in her usual chair, already stitching away at a piece of linen. Enos lay on his belly on the stage, reading. As I approached, Elizabeth dropped her needlework in her lap and sat up straight as a pin, lifting her chin high and pushing her shoulders back as if steeling herself against some sort of attack. She avoided looking directly at me as I got closer.

"Good morning, Mrs. Stutsman," I said, my head drooping like a scolded puppy's. "I wonder if I may speak with you for a moment?"

"Speak away, Mr. Watson," she retorted, still averting her gaze.

"Actually," I said, glancing over at Enos, "I had hoped you would walk with me a moment."

She tightened her lips. "Very well. Enos," she called. "Mr. Watson and I are going to take a stroll. We won't be long." She rose, and I offered my elbow to her. She refused to take it.

"Mrs. Stutsman," I began as we walked down the hall toward the display rooms. "I hope you are well today."

"I am perfectly fine, Mr. Watson, but I don't believe that is what you came here to ask me."

Every word she said made me more nervous. We turned into the cosmorama, and in the dim room surrounded by painted banners, I continued.

"Of course not. Well, I do not mean I do not hope you are well." I cleared my throat. She furrowed her eyebrows, then turned away from me to look into one of the viewing holes.

"Oh! Paris," she said. "I would love to visit France someday."

"Mrs. Stutsman, what I mean to say is, I behaved poorly, no, foolishly last evening. I risked Mr. Dorfoy's reputation by insulting his guest, I ruined what should have been a lovely supper, I set a terrible example for your son, and, worst of all, I treated you with disrespect. Please, I beg your forgiveness."

The candlelight emanating from the viewing holes around the room cast subtle shadows on her face. She began walking again.

"Mr. Watson, it was not your behavior that disturbed me most but its cause. You arrived at supper reeking of whiskey, nearly unable to stand, after I had expressly shared my wishes with you."

"Mrs. Stutsman... please. I know I insulted you. The doctors and myself had a few drinks that afternoon, and I got carried away. Again, please accept my apology."

"And how often do you get carried away, Mr. Watson? If it has happened once, it may as well have happened a hundred times." She stopped walking and turned to face me again.

I looked her in the eyes this time. "You must believe me, Mrs. Stutsman. It is not a regular occurrence." She searched my eyes for a moment until finally her gaze softened.

"It is best to leave whiskey well enough alone. The most enlightened individuals know this. Spirits cloud the mind and destroy the body God has given us. Liquor bankrupts families and ruins homes."

"I am aware of the temperance movement, Mrs. Stutsman, but I believe that in moderation..."

"I do not just follow the movement blindly, Mr. Watson. I have seen liquor's vile qualities with my own eyes and have felt its destructive forces in my own heart." Her voice quaked. She began walking again, and I moved quickly to join her by her side.

"I had no idea it had caused you such pain," I said, offering her my arm. This time, to my surprise, she placed her hand in the crook of my elbow.

"Hans," she began, taking a deep breath, "My brother." We resumed walking. "Hans and I were very close in age. He was born only a year before me. We grew up together, and barely a minute went by that we were not side by side, getting into all sorts of mischief." A quick smile passed over her lips.

"He started school nearby, and mother taught me at home. But we always did our chores together in the afternoons and talked into the night until bedtime."

"He sounds like a wonderful brother," I offered.

"Truly he was. Once, I was reading in the forest near

the path Hans took to school. I was about twelve. Three older boys crept out of the underbrush and started throwing rocks at me. I was terrified, completely frozen and unable to run. Hans heard my scream and came to my rescue. He picked up a large stick and chased the boys down, smacking one of them hard across the back so they knew he meant business. He would never let any harm come to me."

I imagined Elizabeth as a girl, frightened and alone, her sandy hair falling from her bonnet as the terrible boys pelted her with stones. She was still small, not much larger than a girl, but she had hardened over the years. Her nose was thin, her cheekbones high, with no remnants of the plump flesh that fills out a girl's face. She continued talking.

"When he was seventeen, Hans got an offer in town. It was hard work at a lumber mill. Although he was smart and had schooling, our family needed the money so he took the job. At first, he would come home late. Mother would warm his food, and we would talk in the kitchen near the hearth while he ate. Sometimes we would go walking in the evenings, and he would tell me about his day and about his new friends. But he started coming home later and later. I often could not wait up for him. I'd hear the door swing open and slam shut, heavy footsteps, some dishes rattling around, and then silence. I saw him less and less."

"Such things often happen when siblings grow up."

"True, but this was much different. One night, I heard him wretching. I thought he was ill, so I ran to his room to help. He groaned, told me to go away, in such terms I cannot even repeat, and slammed the door in my face. I cried all night long. Why would he say such awful things? After that, he began to sleep late. Mother would beg him to get up. Father would yell and practically push him out the door, but despite their efforts, Hans lost his job at the mill and began pleading with father for money. Father would refuse, but mother would sneak him a bit of change now and then. Although he had no occupation, he would disappear for days at a time and return home to sleep for hours and hours. It was through hearing my parents' disagreements that I came to understand what was happening. 'Stop giving him money,' I heard my father say. 'He is frittering it away on whiskey.' My mother would cry, saying she worried he would starve— he rarely ate at home by this time."

"I cannot imagine the pressure the situation put upon your parents."

"It caused my mother much pain. She cried for nearly the whole of two years. My brother—my protector, my dearest friend—was a stinking drunkard. Finally, my father handed him an ultimatum—he told Hans he must straighten up and find another job or leave immediately."

"What did he do?"

"He left."

"I'm very sorry."

"Wait—that is not all. He left but returned two weeks later. He told us he was no longer drinking and that he saw the error of his ways. He had not yet secured work, but trusting his word, my father spoke to a friend who agreed to hire Hans on a temporary basis."

"So, he found his way out of the darkness."

"He worked for our father's friend for less than a month. During that time, it was as if the old Hans had returned to us. We shared meals and laughed as a family, and he helped father with odd jobs around the house. But the money he earned from his new job had to be spent on something, and he ran into his old friends from the mill in town. One night of hard drinking was enough to send him spiraling down again. Hans came home late one evening, and father asked him to leave. Mother had not yet cleared the table, and Hans swept his arm across it, sending the dishes smashing to the floor. Mother screamed, and my father roared, 'Leave!' Hans raised a fist and attempted to land it on father's face, but his impaired balance gave my father time to intercept the blow. He twisted Hans' arm behind his back and shoved him toward the door. As Hans kicked it open, he yelled, 'Your daughter's a whore!' He disappeared into the night and never returned."

Elizabeth stared off toward the end of the room, obviously not looking at what was before her, but gazing inward, remembering.

"Mrs. Stutsman... Elizabeth," I took a chance saying her given name. "I regret my behavior terribly and do not expect you to ever forgive me."

She looked up at me, her eyes shining with tears. "You could not have known," she said in almost a whisper.

"Is your brother still alive?" I asked cautiously.

"Yes. Besides Enos, Hans is my only living relative. If

you can indeed consider it living—whiskey has killed every shred of kindness in him. He is but a shell of his former self."

We stood there together for a few moments not saying a word. I wanted to take away Elizabeth's sorrow, push it down to the floor, stomp it under my boot. At that moment, I vowed to myself that I'd never drink another drop of hard liquor.

Suddenly, we heard footsteps approaching from down the corridor. We moved a half step apart, and Elizabeth dabbed at her eyes with her handkerchief. She was smoothing her hair when Dorfoy burst into the room.

"There you are, my boy!" he exclaimed. "So very glad I found you. Come, help Thomas and me unload the carriage."

"Mr. Dorfoy," said Elizabeth. "You are safe!" She ran to him and took both his hands in hers. "I cannot express the worry we have all experienced this past day." He must have thought her eyes were red with tears of joy.

"My dear, it was nothing. I reached the collectors' house before the snow began to fall. I dare say, however, when my driver and I tried to walk back to our carriage, the path was so dreadfully covered with ice we could scarcely stand. It was but a thin frozen crust, however, and melted quickly."

"It is good you chose to stay there. The weather was terribly trying here."

"I trust Mr. Watson was helpful to you in my absence?" Dorfoy asked, looking at me. I held my breath, still wondering if Elizabeth had chosen to forgive me.

"Indeed," she replied. "He was quite gracious."

Dorfoy turned his eyes toward Elizabeth then quickly back to me again. "What brings the two of you here?" he asked suspiciously. Elizabeth's face turned pink.

"I wanted to show Mrs. Stutsman the cosmorama."

"Yes," she said. "I had never seen one before. I've decided I must go to Paris someday."

"Absolutely, you must," replied Dorfoy, seemingly relieved. "Has my guest arrived safely?"

"Yes," replied Elizabeth, glancing at me. "Dr. Bell arrived yesterday, and we had a lovely afternoon."

"The weather shut us down," I added. "We were very sorry to have been forced to cancel his first demonstration."

"Fine, fine," said Dorfoy. "Completely understandable. I should like to greet him."

"I believe he is away from the museum for the day, Mr. Dorfoy," I said.

"Ah, very well. I shall see him this evening. Now, Mr. Watson, let us go help Thomas. I've brought back many new things."

The three of us walked out of the darkened room. Sunlight streaming through the clerestory windows had brightened the grand hall. Elizabeth eagerly returned to her chair and picked up her needlework once again.

"Mr. Dorfoy!" called Enos. "I'm glad you are safe."

Dorfoy walked over to the stage. "Still reading, are we?"

"Yes, sir," replied the boy. "I met Mr. Powers today. He is the one who lent me the books."

"Is this true?" Dorfoy asked me.

"Yes, indeed."

"Well, well," Dorfoy smiled and shook his head. "Mr. Powers. I should have guessed as much. As long as you are content, Enos."

"Content, sir? I am more than content. Ichabod Crane has just witnessed a headless figure galloping on a dark horse. I am ecstatic!"

We laughed and turned toward the stairs. As we descended, I said, "It is amazing that Enos comprehends such complicated literature at such a young age."

"Yes, it is. I have said he is a remarkable boy."

"You are very charitable to give Mrs. Stutsman the proceeds from admission so Enos can attend school." I looked at his face to gauge his reaction. He remained expressionless, looking down to focus on the stairs as we reached the first floor.

"Thomas is out front," he said as we approached the entrance hall. I would bring up the subject again later at a more opportune time.

# Chapter 18
## The Greatest Mineral Collection
## in the West

*Arthur Watson*

It was a sunny day with the kind of crisp, blue sky that only appears in winter. Thomas was already unloading the wagon, carrying box after box and placing them near the museum entrance.

"Wagon's empty now, sir," he said. "I'll take it 'round back and unhitch the horses."

"Certainly, Thomas," said Dorfoy. "Mr. Watson, will you start hauling boxes inside? They should be stacked in the third room off the front hall. I'll meet you there." He propped the door open with a brick and went inside.

I nearly wrenched my back when I picked up the first small wooden box, which was much heavier than it appeared. I used my legs to support the weight as I carried it in. "What's in here? A pile of rocks?" I asked Dorfoy when I reached the room.

"Why, yes," he laughed. "You could say that."

Thomas had returned, and he and I made several trips to and from the front of the museum. The muscles in my arms and lower back were burning by the time we finished.

"That oughta do it, boss," said Thomas. "Need help opening 'em?"

"No, Thomas. Mr. Watson and I can take it from here. Thank you."

Thomas touched the brim of his hat, bowed his head to us, and turned to leave. The room was quiet for a moment as Dorfoy and I surveyed the stack of boxes. There were at least thirty small, flat wooden crates.

"Bring the first box here." Dorfoy walked toward a large table near the back of the room.

My arms felt rubbery as I lifted the box and carried it to the table. I set it down in front of Dorfoy, and he pulled a small tool from his coat pocket to pry the lid off. When he removed the pine box top, he revealed a polished mahogany chest inside. He reached his hands around either side of the box and lifted it from the crate.

"The gentleman I visited yesterday sold me his entire collection." Dorfoy opened the hinged lid of the box. Inside, it was sectioned with thin wooden strips into a grid of twenty squares, each holding a gleaming, colorful stone. Dorfoy pushed the box across the table into a shaft of sunlight that shone through the window. The stones glinted purple, green, blue, nearly every color imaginable.

"They're beautiful," I said.

"When combined with those I currently own, they will comprise the greatest mineral collection in the West." Dorfoy's eyes sparkled almost as brightly as the stones.

I considered how much these gems must have cost. I

assumed it was a large price and wondered how he could afford such a purchase when the museum was in financial straits. I still had not been paid. I decided it was not the best time to inquire about this, given Dorfoy's immense excitement over his new acquisition.

"Look at this wonderful example of aquamarine," he said as he lifted a specimen out of the box. A clear, greenish blue shaft jutted from a gray chunk of rock. "And, here is an excellent rose quartz." He placed the aquamarine back into its square chamber and pulled out a pink mass of crystals, raising it to allow the sunlight to shine through.

"Very lovely," I said. We spent the next few hours prying open crates, removing boxes, and examining the contents. Dorfoy used a hand lens to inspect the specimens for damage that might have occurred on their journey.

"I certainly hope I will not find any cracks or fissures," he said, his right eye magnified gigantically in the lens. "It was a bumpy ride. The melting snow produced many wagon ruts in the road." He turned a green stone around and around, looking for imperfections. I did the same with Dorfoy that afternoon, turning him over and over in my mind's eye, trying to uncover his flaws.

# Chapter 19
## Belmont

*Arthur Watson*

D orfoy had instructed me to come to his office later that day to run some errands. When I arrived, my back still aching, he rose from his desk to hand me two small, ivory-colored envelopes. "There is one for Dr. Drake and one for Mr. Longworth. The doctor's office is on Fourth near Vine, and Longworth's is..."

"Yes, sir. I know Mr. Longworth's home by reputation." I was now very nervous. I had never approached such a grand residence.

"Wonderful. You will want to see Dr. Drake first, as he will leave soon for his early evening calls." He sat down and immediately began entering numbers in his ledger.

"Certainly, Mr. Dorfoy." I did not mention I had already visited Dr. Drake's office, as I did not want Dorfoy to think it was my habit to use my work time for personal business.

Dusk approached as I set out on the easy walk to Dr. Drake's. The sun had shone brightly all day, melting much of the snow that had collected on the streets and walks the previous evening, and all along Fourth Street shopkeepers were closing down for the night. Now, as twilight approached, slush and water began to freeze, forming slick patches of ice. I watched my footing, navigating among snow, slush, water, mud, and ice. This precarious state between freeze and thaw signaled the impending spring, but winter had yet another month at least to rear its frigid head.

I had just reached the block on which Dr. Drake's office stood when I noticed a gentleman exit the doctor's office, walk down the steps, and head in my direction. As he got closer, I saw the face beneath the black top hat belonged to Dr. Bell. I was embarrassed to see him.

"Greetings, Mr. Watson," he said.

"Good evening, Dr. Bell."

"I was just on my way to the museum. I hope you will attend my demonstration this evening."

"I am planning on it. I must first finish some errands for Mr. Dorfoy, however."

"Well I hope you will hurry. I am on at seven."

"I will certainly return by then." I bowed my head slightly, and continued, "Please accept my apology, Dr. Bell, if I offended you at supper yesterday." I attempted to keep walking toward Dr. Drake's.

"Wait, Mr. Watson."

"Yes?"

"Mrs. Stutsman, Enos, and I will dine with Mr. Dorfoy after the demonstration. You are welcome to join us if you wish."

"Thank you, Dr. Bell. I shall consider it." Perplexed by

his gracious invitation in light of my insulting behavior the day before, I rushed past him down the sidewalk.

The same student who had helped me on my last visit answered the doctor's door. "I have a delivery for Dr. Drake," I said. "Will you make sure he receives it before he leaves?"

"Yes, sir." He took the letter from me and closed the door.

I retraced my steps and headed east on Fourth Street. I had never ventured beyond the business district and grew exceedingly nervous as the number of buildings began to thin, giving way to a few grand townhouses. Longworth's home, Belmont, stood on Pike Street at the end of Fourth Street. I could already see it up ahead in the purple glow of the approaching twilight. Skeletons of grape vines stretched in rows up the distant, snow-covered hill behind the house. A garden shrouded in snow and punctuated with leafless fruit trees surrounded the mansion. Belmont's white façade resembled a Greek temple. A portico framed its entrance, flanked with two columns on each side. Two tall windows rose on either side of the portico, with small windows directly below them at ground level and oval windows that looked like flattened wagon wheels above. The pediment above the doors held another oval window with spokes that radiated from its center.

The paved path leading to the entrance had been cleared of snow and ice. I climbed the stairs that led to the door and paused to straighten my hat and scarf before reaching for the heavy brass doorknocker. I knocked three times and waited. After a few moments, I knocked again, knowing it could take some time for Longworth's servants to hear the knock and make their way through the sprawling house. Just as I reached for the knocker again, the door creaked open. A disheveled man wearing an ill-fitting brown suit stood in the doorway. His hair was as overgrown as the gardens around the house, and his sideburns and eyebrows sprouted wildly from his head.

"How may I help you?" he asked.

"Good evening," I replied. "I bring a letter for the man of the house."

"Ah! Certainly. Won't you come in?" He opened the door further, stepping aside and gesturing for me to enter.

The doorway opened to a grand foyer with parlors on either side. Large paintings and marble sculptures lined the hallway. I looked up to see a grand medallion of acanthus leaves in the center of the ceiling, from which hung an elaborate chandelier. The strange man, who must have been the butler, shuffled out of the foyer, into the hallway, and out of sight.

He suddenly emerged from around the corner, his abrupt reappearance startling me.

"Please," he asked, "won't you wait in here?"

He led me into one of the parlors, gestured toward a stuffed chair, and disappeared once again into the hallway. A roaring fire warmed the room, and candles flickered on the tables and mantel. A book lay open on the table before the sofa, and when I leaned over for a better look, I saw it contained horticultural illustrations.

The man returned, and I rose from my chair. "So," he said, "I understand you have a message for Mr. Longworth."

"Yes, I do," I replied.

"And you are?"

"Arthur Watson, on behalf of Joseph Dorfoy."

The man extended his hand. "Pleased to meet you, Mr. Watson." I noticed that on his sleeve he had pinned small pieces of paper scrawled with writing.

Puzzled, I shook his hand and replied, "Pleased to meet you as well." He must have noticed my quick attention to the notes, because he explained, "Many, many important things to remember!"

We stood there silently a moment until the man said, "Well, where is my letter then?" He looked at me anxiously.

"Your letter, sir?" I asked. I was completely confused, when suddenly my stomach dropped. Sweat immediately burst from my forehead. I swallowed hard.

"Why yes," he replied. "I am Nicholas Longworth."

"Beg pardon, sir. Of course." I tried to cover my error and fumbled into my pocket to pull out the envelope. Longworth took it from me and sat on the sofa.

"Please, sit awhile," he said kindly, driving away my awkwardness with his disarming smile. "My wife and children are away on a family visit, and the house feels so empty without them."

I sat down in a chair facing Longworth. "Mr. Dorfoy shared some of your wine with me, Mr. Longworth," I said. "I found it quite good, and he was very proud it had been made right here."

"I appreciate your compliment, Mr. Watson. Dorfoy is such a gracious friend, but I have yet to perfect that wine. It took me years to grow grapes in this soil, and my first attempts at fermentation turned out bitter sludge. I tried removing the grape skins, which improved the taste significantly, but it's not quite right. Very dry. Definitely not equal to its European counterpart, but I shall not give up. There are many Germans here who cannot get enough of it, so I must be close." He opened the envelope, pulled out the letter, and unfolded it. "So, what does old Dorfoy have to say? He is just down the street— he could have paid me a visit himself." He narrowed his eyes and began to read. "Hmm. Well. I see..."

I found it unusual that he had not read the letter in private, but I quietly waited for him to finish. Once he had, he put the letter down on the table and looked up at me. I was a bit anxious about what had been so urgent that Dorfoy needed the letters delivered immediately.

"I think I shall have a dinner party."

"Pardon me, sir?"

"A dinner party. As I said, I am lonely without my family, and they will not return for another week." He stood up, obviously excited by his idea. "My dear friend Mr. Powers has told me about the precocious young boy who is currently at the museum. Do you think he would honor me with his presence?"

"I don't see why not, sir. Of course, it will be his mother's decision, but I believe both she and Enos would be delighted."

"Please extend my invitation to the boy, his mother, and Mr. Dorfoy. Oh, heavens, of course you must also come! I will request Mr. Powers' and his wife's presence myself. Seven o'clock tomorrow night. Sunday evening is a wonderful time for dinner with friends, is it not?"

"Certainly, Mr. Longworth." I stood up to take my leave. "The museum shall be closed for the evening, so it will be the perfect time." He saw me to the door.

"Good evening, Mr. Watson. I look forward to seeing you again soon."

"Good night, Mr. Longworth."

I had not expected Mr. Longworth's demeanor. He was much unlike his formal, stately, and intimidating home. He was casual, forthright, and even a bit frumpy. I enjoyed him tremendously and looked forward to tomorrow evening.

The big door creaked closed, and I headed down the front steps into the night. Darkness had blanketed the city while I was inside Belmont, and it was much darker here than near the business district. Only a few townhouses stood along the dirt road, and soft lamplight and the flicker of fireplaces warmed their windows. It had also grown much colder, so I tightened my scarf around my neck, fastened the top button of my coat, and trudged back to the museum.

# Chapter 20
## Dr. Bell's Demonstration

*Arthur Watson*

I hurried into the nearly full theater to find Elizabeth and Enos already seated near the stage. She noticed me enter and motioned for me to come over. As I walked down the aisle, Mr. Powers called my name. He introduced me to his wife, and I greeted them both quickly but cordially before continuing on toward Elizabeth.

"Dr. Bell reserved seats for us," she said when I arrived, "and we held this one for you." She gestured to the empty chair next to Enos.

"What a shame that the weather disrupted Dr. Bell's first performance yesterday evening," I said, not sure if I really meant it.

"Actually, Mr. Dorfoy asked him to stay for one more demonstration on Monday," Elizabeth said, "since he made the long trip here, and because Mr. Dorfoy had promised the public two demonstrations. So, he shall be in town for a few more days."

"Well, isn't that terrific," I said.

"Here he comes now," said Elizabeth.

Dr. Bell strode in through the door. His posture was

unbelievably straight, making him seem taller than anyone else in the room. He removed his hat and looked around the theater, obviously seeking someone out in the crowd. Once he noticed Elizabeth, his eyes focused on her face. He did not divert them until he stood directly in front of her, took her hand in his, raised it to his lips, and kissed it. Elizabeth blushed, and Enos giggled. I just stared in disbelief.

"Good evening, Mrs. Stutsman," said Dr. Bell. "You look lovely tonight."

Elizabeth looked down at the floor. "Good evening, Dr. Bell," she said. "Thank you for reserving us such prime seats."

"I wanted you and Enos to have the best view possible for my demonstration," he said, smiling. "Oh, hello, Mr. Watson. I see you shall be sitting in this row as well."

"Yes," chimed Enos. "We saved him a chair."

"How kind of you." Bell turned to me. "I hope you'll find my demonstration of interest. Now, if you'll excuse me, I must step backstage to prepare." He bowed to Elizabeth, turned, and disappeared into a small doorway to the left of the stage.

"He's a mysterious man, isn't he?" asked Elizabeth.

"About as mysterious as a charlatan," I replied.

"Mr. Watson!" she retorted, and I could see that she intended to scold me further until she was interrupted by music piping from the huge organ at the side of the theater. Dorfoy, that jack-of-all-trades, played it himself. The melody swirled up around us, eerie and strange, its discordant sounds startling and invigorating at the same time. When he finished, the audience applauded as he stepped onto the stage, which was framed with ornate gilded plaster and hung at the back with a heavy red curtain.

"Welcome, dear friends," Dorfoy bellowed. "I am happy we could accommodate those of you who held tickets for last evening's event. I am also pleased to announce that I have scheduled one more demonstration by Dr. Bell for Monday evening, since his first was cancelled due to the inclement weather."

The theater was full. People even stood at the back. All were silent, their attention focused on Dorfoy.

"And now, you are in for a truly amazing evening. I bring to you Dr. Damien Bell, direct from Boston, who has studied the science of phrenology with the best practitioners in the East. Dr. Bell possesses the uncanny ability to reveal a person's true nature by examining the shape of his skull. He will do so tonight with the help of subjects selected from among you, our wonderful audience. I must caution that if you are attempting to hide something, you would do best to avoid coming onto the stage." Laughter rose from the audience.

"Without further ado, I present to you Dr. Damien Bell, phrenologist."

The audience applauded as the red curtain opened. I noticed the light dimmed, and I turned around to see Thomas and Ginny dousing some of the lamps and candles around the seating area. The stage itself was lit brightly enough to illuminate two large banners that hung from the ceiling at the back. They were each covered with a simple line drawing of a head, one a profile, the other a frontal view. Each head was divided into sections, with words filling each subdivision. The audience began to whisper when footsteps came out of the darkness behind the drawings. Dr. Bell emerged from between the two banners, and the crowd applauded. He bowed, then walked to the front edge of the stage and stared intensely into the audience.

"Human nature. Faculties. Sentiments. Propensities. Character," he said, his voice booming throughout the theater. "What are they exactly, and where do they originate? Are they within the body? The heart?" He tapped his chest with his hand. "Or do they reside within the mind? And what is the mind? Where is the mind?" Bell turned quickly, his coat swirling out behind him. He pointed to the drawing on the right. "Science is just beginning to unlock these mysteries."

I glanced over at Elizabeth. Both she and Enos were enthralled.

"The brain is known to play a role in determining who we are and how we behave." Bell continued as he pointed again to the drawing. "Housed within the skull, the brain itself is composed of organs that control different aspects of our mind."

"Countless experiments and observations have delivered our modern ideas about the mind. The ancient Greeks, particularly Aristotle, placed importance on bodily organs, such as the liver, in determining personality and character. But new thinkers in Europe, especially the German physicians Gall and more recently

Spurzheim—my recently deceased teacher, God rest his soul—have determined the brain's significance through careful study over the course of many years."

"You see on these charts the basics of phrenology. However, examination of the skull must be conducted by a professional such as myself who can provide the correct interpretation of his findings. There are very few of us in existence in this country as of now; however, many men purport to possess the skills to conduct a proper phrenological reading. Beware these itinerant hacks who prey on people for profit."

"Many of my patients have testified that my examinations helped them make important decisions in their lives, such as when to invest, where to travel, and even whom to marry. But that is not my ultimate goal. I do not condone phrenology as a form of fortune telling. I simply wish to reveal to the individual his true character so he may better know himself." He walked again to the front of the stage. "Now, where shall we begin?"

Bell surveyed the audience. Several men raised their hands, surprisingly eager to be examined in front of their peers.

"You, in the back," Bell pointed at one of the men.

The audience cheered the man as he walked up the aisle. Bell pulled a chair to the center of the stage and asked him to be seated.

"What is your name, sir?" asked Bell.

"I am Mr. Morgan. Mr. John Morgan."

Dorfoy stepped up on stage carrying a small table with a leather case on top of it, placed the table next to the chair, and left the stage without a word.

"I am pleased to make your acquaintance Mr. Morgan. You are a brave man to expose your inner self before your friends, your family, and your colleagues."

"I assure you, I have nothing to hide," said Mr. Morgan, pushing up his spectacles. He was tall and firmly built, with dark hair grayed at the temples. Well-dressed and well-groomed, he had a cosmopolitan air about him.

"Allow me to explain what I am about to do." Bell pulled a metal instrument from the leather case. Mr. Morgan jumped, and Bell pushed him back down by his shoulder. "Not to worry, sir. This is simply a measuring device. It will not hurt a bit." The audience roared with laughter as Mr. Morgan let out a sigh of relief. "First, I shall complete detailed measurements of your skull." Bell placed the ends the instrument, which opened with handles like a scissors, on each of Mr. Morgan's temples, and then jotted some figures down on a piece of paper. He then wrapped a tape around the man's head directly above his eyebrows, again recording the measurements.

"Next, I will feel your skull for areas that are either raised or depressed, and chart them accordingly." Bell placed his hands on Mr. Morgan's head in the same manner he had done with Elizabeth that day in the dining room. He closed his eyes, seeming to concentrate deeply, as his fingers ruffled through the man's hair. The audience remained silent, transfixed by this strange activity they had never seen before.

"There!" said Bell. "I do believe I have finished. Please, stay seated, Mr. Morgan, as I share my reading with you and the rest of the audience."

Mr. Morgan looked a bit nervous. "I certainly hope your findings are positive." He shifted in his chair.

"Well, first of all, I believe you are very confident. You are comfortable with some risk but only that which has potential benefit. You are idealistic—I dare say, a do-gooder. You possess strong powers of concentration. And, you are very firm-handed, but at times this trait will appear to be combativeness. You should pay close attention to control this."

Mr. Morgan looked surprised. "I am amazed at what a close picture you paint of me. I am a businessman, and I must use all these things in my daily negotiations. Thank you, Dr. Bell. I will take your advice to heart." He stood up, and the audience applauded.

I could have guessed these things about the man just by looking at him, I thought to myself as he returned to his seat. His manner of dress and comportment suggested a successful businessman, all of whom are usually confident, firm, focused, and idealistic. The show had been entertaining none the less.

"Who would like to be next?" asked Bell. His eyes scanned the crowd. Several people, all men, raised their hands. It would have been improper on several accounts for a woman to volunteer. The audience waited for Bell to select his next subject, and despite the many willing souls, his eyes alighted on me.

"How about you, Mr. Watson?"

I swallowed hard and looked back to the eager gentlemen who had been snubbed, as if to say, "But, Dr.

Bell, what about them?"

"Well, Mr. Watson? Don't be shy. Let's give him a round of applause."

Every inch of my body, every hair of my head, would have preferred to stay right in my seat. I had never felt such aversion to standing up before in my life.

"Go on, Mr. Watson," said Enos, tugging on my sleeve. What could I do?

Engulfed in the audience's clapping, I stood up and made my way onto the stage. Bell gestured toward the chair, and I sat down. In front of me, the audience was dark, but I could make out the shapes of at least a hundred faces watching me, anxious to delve into the recesses of my mind. My heart beat wildly, nearly leaping into my throat. I felt beads of sweat rise up on my forehead. Calm yourself, Arthur! I could not appear nervous before this man, lest he win this war of wills.

"I will follow the same procedure," said Bell, looking directly into my eyes. The metal instruments felt cold against my temples, and his fingers brushed my nose as he circled my head with the measuring tape. Bell stretched his arms out in front of him, clasped his fingers, turned his palms toward the audience, and cracked his knuckles before placing his hands on my head. I took a deep breath and closed my eyes. He pressed his fingers into the back of my skull firmly, then dragged them lightly across my temples. He ran his index finger from the middle of my forehead to the nape of my neck. He rested his palms on either side of my head, the tips of his fingers touching at the top of my scalp, as if forming an imaginary cap. He held my reputation, quite literally, in his hands. Then, just as suddenly as he began, his arms fell to his sides.

The next few silent, agonizing moments seemed an eternity. I could hear my own pulse throbbing inside my ears.

"Fascinating," said Bell. "I've not yet seen this kind of reading."

I looked up at him incredulously, nearly begging him for mercy.

"You are very cautious, Mr. Watson, and often afraid. You tend to imitate rather than invent. Your will is weak, and you lack the ability to influence others."

I should have predicted this. I could storm off the stage but did not want to offend Mr. Dorfoy or look even more foolish than I already did. I felt hundreds of eyes boring into me. I could see Elizabeth's face, and she cringed after every word Bell uttered.

"Your naivete leads you to make rash decisions," Bell continued, "and you lack the ability to sustain personal relationships. I see other traits, as well, that I would expect to encounter in a woman, but in a man..."

It was as if my body was strapped into the chair. I physically could not move. A few uncomfortable laughs rose from the audience.

"Friends, I assure you, this is a very serious matter," said Bell, with mock concern. "Mr. Watson is yet a very young man, perhaps just about twenty. He has some time to develop his character, but it will be a challenge, for such traits are difficult to completely reverse."

At this point, I felt a surge of strength in my legs. I stood up and walked off the stage, speechless. I approached the row where my chair stood vacant, and saw Elizabeth and Enos looking stunned. For a second, I contemplated sitting down and forgetting what had just happened, but my legs just kept moving. I don't even remember leaving the theatre and exiting the museum. One moment I was in the dim aisle amidst whispers and jeers, the next I was in the cold night air walking in the direction of the river.

As I walked slowly, gazing down at the cobblestones, I heard the quick clicking of footsteps closing in on me. I turned to see a small figure running toward me and suddenly recognized her form.

"Mrs. Stutsman!" I called. "You should not be out here alone."

"I had to see if you were all right," she said, breathlessly, her chest heaving up and down. "You were as pale as death when you left the theater."

"It is cold. You must return immediately." Her bare arms glowed white in the moonlight. I removed my coat and draped it over her shoulders. "Come, I'll see you back to the museum."

We began walking the short distance back to the building. A couple likely out for some Saturday evening entertainment watched us and whispered. They must have seen Elizabeth running after me.

"You mustn't take Dr. Bell's analysis to heart," she said. "I am certain he meant no harm. It was merely a parlor trick."

"Dr. Bell is well respected and certainly the first phrenologist to roll through Cincinnati. I cannot imagine those in the audience would not believe his every word."

"True. But even if he were correct, you are young, and there is time to perfect your flaws. He said so himself. None of us is beyond improvement."

As we approached the front entrance to the museum, people were pouring out the doors. It appeared Dr. Bell had made me his grand finale.

"Mrs. Stutsman, you are blind to the real matter at hand. Whether or not Dr. Bell's words were true, he has essentially ruined my reputation." I paused for a moment, then bowed deeply. "And now, madam, I bid you goodnight." I left her standing there, still wearing my coat around her shoulders.

# Chapter 21
# Looking for Mr. Watson

*Elizabeth Stutsman*

Arthur left me standing there in the cold. He simply turned and walked off into the darkness. I had not considered how my running after him must have looked, but Dr. Bell's every word had filled my heart with pain. I knew Arthur to be a kind person, despite his flaws, and he did not deserve such public humiliation. Perhaps Dr. Bell intended to help him. Knowing one's self intimately is truly the only way to improve one's character. I can only guess what ran through people's minds when I flew from my chair and whipped up the aisle. I'm certain they saw more than concern at work. And now, here I stood with his coat wrapped around my shoulders. I moved away from the doors, trying not to draw attention to myself. Once the crowd had ceased to exit the building, I went inside.

Enos was still in the theater. He had not moved from his seat.

"Mama!" he cried, eyes full of worry. "Why did you leave like that? Did you find Mr. Watson?"

I removed Arthur's coat and draped it over my arm. "Yes, dear. Mr. Watson looked very ill, so I wanted to be certain he was safe."

"Why did Dr. Bell say those things? Why were people laughing?"

"Enos," I said to calm him, "I assure you, Dr. Bell was only trying to help. People come here to be entertained. Most of them likely believe the whole thing very humorous, not anything serious at all."

Enos contemplated this. "I did not find it funny, Mama. Mr. Watson is my friend."

"And mine, too. Dr. Bell will most definitely have an explanation. Now, let's go and get cleaned up." I lifted him from his chair, and we left the theater.

We first passed Arthur's room, and I hung his coat on the doorknob. It was too long and the wool brushed the floor. I did my best to arrange it neatly, so as not to wrinkle the material, before continuing on to our chambers.

"Please dress for supper, Enos." I put him down, opened his door, and walked inside to light a few candles. "I'll call for you when Dr. Bell arrives, and the three of us shall dine with Mr. Dorfoy this evening."

"What about Mr. Watson?" he asked.

"I believe he may wish to dine alone tonight."

I closed the door behind me and went to my room next door. Inside, I had laid out a blue dress, intending to shed my mourning clothes for the first time in nearly a year. Not tonight, I thought, and placed the dress back in my trunk for another time. I splashed water on my face, sat in the chair, leaned my head back, closed my eyes, and waited. It was not more than a few minutes before I heard a knock at the door. I took a deep breath, stood up, and answered it.

"Greetings, Mrs. Stutsman," said Dr. Bell, bowing slightly.

I curtsied without saying a word.

"I trust you are still joining us for supper?" he asked.

"Of course, but we must get Enos first."

I pulled the door shut behind me and knocked on Enos's door. There was no answer. "Come now, son." I knocked again. Still nothing. I opened the door to find the candles extinguished and the room empty.

"Where has he gone?" asked Dr. Bell.

"I cannot believe this," I said. "He has done this before but never after dark."

"I never thought him to be an obstinate child," said Dr. Bell. "You really must try to control such behavior, Mrs. Stutsman."

"My son is missing, Dr. Bell. It is hardly the time to assess his behavior."

He looked at me sheepishly. "You are right. Please forgive me. He must be somewhere nearby. How far could he have gone in his condition?"

"His condition? He is not an invalid, doctor. You would be surprised."

"It appears I am saying all the wrong things. Just stay calm. I shall get some light," said Dr. Bell as he went inside my room to bring out the lamp. "You say he has run off before?"

"I would not call it running off. He is a very curious child and likes to explore the museum on his own."

"You must have some inclination as to where he might be."

I really did not. "I do wish Mr. Watson were here. He knows all of Enos's favorite places."

"Well, Watson is not here," replied Dr. Bell, "So we must start out on our own. Come, take the lamp, and I'll get another candle." Ginny had already extinguished all the lights for the evening, and it was very dark. Dr. Bell emerged from my room, his face flickering in the yellow light from the candle. "First we must go by Mr. Dorfoy's office and alert him to the matter."

We hurried down the hall and up the stairs to Mr. Dorfoy's office.

"What do you mean, the boy is missing?" Mr. Dorfoy asked, looking concerned as he put on his spectacles.

"We mean he was not in his room when we called him for supper," answered Dr. Bell. "Mrs. Stutsman says he has done this before."

"Is this true, Mrs. Stutsman?" asked Mr. Dorfoy.

"Yes, sir. You know his adventurous spirit. He sometimes steals away from his room but only in the mornings. He has never disappeared at night."

"Well, he must be somewhere in the building. Ginny!" called Mr. Dorfoy.

"Sir?" She appeared out of the room adjacent to the office where she was preparing our meal. "Sir? What is the matter?"

"Enos is missing. Find Thomas and ask for his help."

"Ach du liebe! Thomas is just up the hall." She curtsied and quickly left the room.

"I think we should divide," said Dr. Bell. "We can cover the entire building more quickly that way."

"Good idea," said Mr. Dorfoy. "Bell, you take the downstairs east wing. I'll take the west wing."

Ginny returned with Thomas.

"Thomas and Ginny can cover upstairs. Mrs. Stutsman," he said, putting his hand on my shoulder. "Perhaps you should just rest here. You look a bit peaked."

"I assure you, Mr. Dorfoy, that there is nothing I would rather do than look for my son. I am feeling quite strong."

"Very good, then. You shall accompany Ginny upstairs."

Dr. Bell walked over to me, took my hand in both of his, and looked me straight in the eye. "Do not worry," he said. "We shall find him."

"Blasted darkness," said Mr. Dorfoy. "If I could only invest in gas lighting. Peale's Philadelphia museum has gas lights..." He grumbled as he collected the lamp, and then he and Dr. Bell rushed out the door.

"Don't fret, ma'am," said Thomas. "Enos is a good boy. He won't have gone far."

"I'm not so sure, Thomas. I have a strange feeling tonight."

The three of us left Mr. Dorfoy's office. Thomas agreed to search the areas not open to the public, and Ginny and I headed toward the grand hall. It was eerily quiet.

"Enos!" I called, my voice echoing around the high

ceiling. No answer. "Enos!"

Ginny scurried in and out of rooms adjoining the hall. I poked my head into the cosmorama but knew he would not be there. The candles behind the views were out, so he could see nothing of Paris, Rome, or New York. Even so, I called out his name into the dark space.

Ginny and I met in the middle of the grand hall near the small stage where Enos spent his days.

"Ma'am, I'm sorry," she said. "He is not here."

Almost simultaneously we turned our heads toward the back of the hall to the double doors that led to the Infernal Regions.

"Surely he would not have ventured there," I said.

Ginny swallowed nervously. "I'm not going up those stairs with just the two of us, Mrs. Stutsman."

"Oh, Ginny. Don't be silly. There's nothing up there but wax figures."

"I'll go find Thomas," she said, and hurried off without waiting for my response.

I paced for a few seconds. "This is ridiculous!" I said aloud to no one but myself and then walked toward the doors. Just as my hand began to turn the doorknob, Ginny returned with Thomas.

"Agh, no ma'am," he called. "Let me look up there. It's very dark, and not knowin' your way 'round you're likely to stumble and hurt somethin'."

"I want to come, too," I pleaded.

"Now, Mrs. Stutsman. You just sit yourself down on that chair over there and wait for me." He pleaded with me, his eyes surrounded by wrinkles.

"Fine. But I'm not moving until you come back."

Ginny stood firm. "I'll stay here with Mrs. Stutsman."

I sat down in the chair in which I had sat for the past few days. It seemed much later than it really was. I was tired and glanced over at the stage, only able to make out its edges in the darkness. That is where my son spends his time, I thought. I'd run away, too.

Thomas came through the doors a short while later. He looked at me and shook his head.

"Not there, Mrs. Stutsman. I'm sorry."

"I'm grateful for your help, Thomas," I said. "You have been very kind to us."

He crouched down beside me, first tightening his mouth, then taking a deep breath and letting it out slowly. Then he said, "You think he mighta gone lookin' for Mr. Watson?"

I gasped for air. "We must tell Mr. Dorfoy and Dr. Bell right away." I jumped up but had to sit back down. My heart raced and dizziness whirled in my head.

"I'll go tell 'em," said Thomas.

"No—," I replied. "Help me up. I'm coming with you."

Mr. Dorfoy and Dr. Bell met us on our way down the stairs. The minute we saw each other, we knew Enos was not inside the museum.

"He's not here," I said, "but I may know where he went."

I rushed past them to Enos's room. Once inside, I was certain. His coat was missing, as were the mittens I had made for him. He had gone in search of Arthur. The men had followed me to the room, and when I turned to them, they stared at me quizzically.

"He's gone out to find Mr. Watson," I said.

"Heavens!" said Mr. Dorfoy. "Thomas, ready my horse. Bell, you should head out immediately on foot."

I interrupted their frantic conversation. "Walk toward the river. You will probably find Mr. Watson there, and he can help us find Enos."

Dr. Bell turned to me. "How do you know Watson's whereabouts?" he asked.

"Does it really matter?" barked Mr. Dorfoy.

"Of course not." Dr. Bell put his hand on my shoulder. "We will find him, Mrs. Stutsman."

The three men headed toward the front doors. The corridor was dark, but I felt safety emanating from the shadows. Outside, danger lurked everywhere. Thieves, beggars, drunkards stumbling out of taverns, women of ill repute. My heart pounded, my stomach churned. This was all my fault. We should have never come here.

# Chapter 22
## The Public Landing

*Arthur Watson*

I probably should have taken my coat back from Elizabeth. My arms were beginning to sting, and I crossed them in front of me and rubbed my shoulders to warm myself. But I could not go back just yet. I was still not sure how I would face Dorfoy, and I needed to think about what had happened. I knew Bell had designs on Elizabeth and for some reason felt it necessary to destroy me in the process. I found Elizabeth fascinating, but we were only friends, and mostly because of Enos. The boy was at the center of it all, and I was most concerned with his feelings. He had sat in the audience as well while Bell tore apart every respectable feature of my character. Perhaps Bell spoke the truth. I shook my head, knowing this could not be the case.

I reached the public landing and walked along the river. The place was nearly deserted, save for some commotion from one of the taverns on Front Street. Loud voices and music carried through the night air, merry sounds that floated out over the water. I stopped at a stack of boards someone had left from earlier in the day and sat down. Looking over the river toward

Kentucky into the darkness black as pitch, my head began to clear. It crossed my thoughts that someone in a more precarious state of mind might consider throwing himself into the river, letting the frigid water obliterate him as if he had never existed.

Something tugged at me, however, that would not allow this option. I could leave Cincinnati for another city or for the frontier that lay west or south, like the land beyond the river. But, I knew I was not cut out for that kind of life. There were things here that required attention. I was not the kind of man Bell had described. Yet, he had such power over people. I saw the way Dr. Drake had pondered his ideas and how Dorfoy catered to his every need. Mostly, I saw how his eyes burned into Elizabeth and the way she tittered and went weak when he kissed her hand. Anger welled up in my chest, fueling the feeling that something was very, very wrong.

I stood up and began walking away from the river when I heard a distant child's voice. There, at the end of a short dock just upstream, I saw the silhouette of a small figure against the moonlight reflecting off the water.

"Mr. Watson?" I heard the figure call.

"Enos?" I yelled. "Stay right there!"

He turned toward my voice, and I sprinted toward him. As I reached the water's edge, Enos started moving back to shore. I saw him plant his hands and swing his torso between them, but as he landed, he slipped and tumbled over the edge. I hurtled myself onto the dock and nearly lost my footing on its ice-covered surface. Enos struggled in the frigid water below, close to shore yet unable to reach it. Without thinking, I threw myself in after him.

Chunks of ice grazed my arms and neck. By the time I grabbed the boy's collar, he had stopped thrashing. I dragged him to shore and saw a figure there. It was dark, my head was foggy with cold, so I did not recognize him.

"Hand me the boy!" he called.

I pushed Enos, limp and pathetic, toward the man, who scooped him up. As I struggled to my feet, the man kicked me hard in the chest. The blow took my breath away as if my lungs had been crushed. I fell back into the water, and when I regained my composure and dragged myself from the river, he and Enos were gone.

# Chapter 23
## The Rescue

*Elizabeth Stutsman*

Ginny and I paced the entrance corridor until we heard the front doors swing open. I thought my heart would burst from my chest when I saw the figure's silhouette, and rushed to the man who held a drooping bundle in his arms. It was Dr. Bell with Enos, soaking wet and wrapped in his coat.

I felt Enos's forehead and cheeks. They were cold and pale.

"Mama," Enos said weakly.

"He's freezing. We must get him to his room," said Dr. Bell. "Thomas is already fetching Dr. Drake."

I followed him to Enos's room, where we stripped off his wet clothes and placed him in bed. I pulled his quilt over him, the same quilt that kept him warm on his journey to Cincinnati.

"Light the stove, Ginny. We will need more wood. Dr. Bell, please get more blankets from my room," I said, tucking the quilt tightly around my boy's small body. Dr. Bell quickly returned and piled the other blankets on top.

"I found him lying in an alley near the river, wet and unconscious," said Dr. Bell.

"You brought my son home to me. I owe you my life." I sat on the floor beside Enos's bed, legs curled under my skirt, and brushed a lock of hair away from his eyes.

"What were you thinking, Enos?" I asked.

"When you said Mr. Watson would not be dining with us, I got worried about him. I couldn't find him anywhere in the museum. I'm sorry I fell in the river."

"You shouldn't have gone out alone," I continued, stroking his hair.

"Are you angry with me, Mama?" he asked.

"Oh, Enos, how could I be angry? I am happy you are safe. Now, stay quiet and rest. Dr. Drake will be here soon." He turned over onto his side and closed his eyes, his breaths long and deep.

Ginny returned with more wood and placed it in the stove. The fire blazed, filling the room with a strong, rich heat that penetrated our clothes.

"Perhaps we should leave you and Enos alone, Mrs. Stutsman. The boy needs to rest," she said.

"Thank you both for your help. There's nothing else you can do right now."

Just as they prepared to leave, Thomas and Mr. Dorfoy arrived with Dr. Drake.

"You'll all need to give us some room," the doctor said.

"We were just on our way out," said Dr. Bell. "Come, Mrs. Stutsman." He put his arm around my shoulders to steady me.

As we left the room, I turned to see Dr. Drake open his bag and lean over Enos. I shut the door behind me.

"I rode as quick as I could," said Thomas.

"You did very well," said Mr. Dorfoy, patting him on the back.

"Sure hope nothin' happens to him. He's such a nice boy," Thomas continued.

The four of us waited outside Enos's room. We said not a word as the time passed. Ginny put her ear to the door.

"I don't hear anything," she said. "It's quiet. What is the doctor doing in there?"

We had no answers, but continued milling around in the hallway until the door finally opened. All of us gathered around Dr. Drake, looking at him expectantly.

"Well?" I finally asked, "How is he?"

The doctor paused a moment, and I felt my heart drop. Then a kind smile grew across his face.

"He's going to be just fine," he said.

A collective sigh heaved from all our chests.

"There are no signs of permanent damage from the cold, no hypothermia nor indication of fever or consumption. I could hear no water in his lungs. He is simply suffering from the shock of it all. I treated him, and he should recover within a day or two from his exhaustion."

I felt a huge weight lift from me.

"Now," continued the doctor, "I suggest you all return to your quarters. The boy needs his rest, as does his mother."

"Thank heavens you found him," said Ginny, turning to Dr. Bell.

"Perhaps this would have not happened had Mr. Watson not stormed off in such a rash manner," said Dr. Bell.

"Bell," said Mr. Dorfoy. "This is hardly Mr. Watson's fault. Has he not yet returned?"

"No, he has not," I answered.

"I will pay a visit in the morning to ensure you are well, Mrs. Stutsman. In the meantime, please call for me at the hotel should something go amiss."

"We will certainly do so, Dr. Bell," said Mr. Dorfoy. "The rest of you, get some sleep. Thank you once again, Dr. Drake."

"Please send for me if the boy's condition changes," said the doctor. "He is fortunate you found him when you did, Dr. Bell."

# Chapter 24
## Arthur's Return

*Arthur Watson*

I pounded on Elizabeth's door, my muscles and joints slow and aching.

"Elizabeth!"

The door to Enos's room, which was directly next to Elizabeth's, opened quickly. "Arthur... Mr. Watson," she whispered, stepping into the hall. "Enos is sleeping. Hush!" She touched my arm. "Heavens! You're drenched and freezing." She steered me down the hall toward my own chamber.

My coat hung neatly on the doorknob, and Elizabeth removed it and wrapped it around my shoulders as my teeth chattered. Her scent still lingered on its collar, a faint floral bouquet that might have been violets or lavender.

"We must get you warm," she said as she hurried over to the stove to light it.

"Enos. Is he safe?"

"He's resting. He's fine."

"Where's Bell?"

"Dr. Bell carried him back here. Mr. Watson, what happened to you?"

"Bell took him. From the river." I struggled to explain. "I don't understand. Dr. Bell found him in an alley."

I fought hard to remember what had occurred. I knew that I had jumped in to rescue Enos, and that a man had taken him from me.

"Bell tried to kill me! He knocked me back into the water."

"Arthur, calm down," she whispered. "You're confused. You're cold and not thinking clearly."

I was chilled to the bone. I removed my coat and immediately began unbuttoning my wet shirt. Elizabeth turned her back to me as I quickly stripped.

"Right. You need to get out of those clothes," she said awkwardly as I climbed into bed. "Don't worry about Enos. He will be as good as new in the morning." Shivering, I drifted off to the sound of her voice, soft as the feathers in my pillow.

I awoke in the middle of the night and could not sleep. Wrapped in my blanket, I began to walk back and forth, hoping it would warm away the last bit of chill. My foot brushed something on the floor—a letter that someone had slid under the door. It must have arrived in the post that day, but I had not been back to my room since morning. I turned it over and recognized the handwriting immediately. It was from my brother, Harold. The flourish that crossed the "t"s and the tall, pointed "w", both so similar to my penmanship, comforted me. It was the first letter I had received from my family, so I sat on the bed and opened it right away.

*Dear Arthur,*

*I hope this letter finds you well, and that you have secured work and will soon achieve the place you deserve in a prosperous profession. Mother and Father are well, as are Penny, Miranda, and Catherine. We are, however, impatiently waiting spring. It has been very cold, and the girls are beginning to make us insane with their complaining. A young man has begun calling for Penny, and Father is not happy about it. He says she is too young, and I have to agree, she having just turned fifteen. He does seem nice enough, though. I have been helping Father before and after school each day, and am learning more about the farm. I pray he will give me more responsibilities once I turn eighteen in May. Our mare is pregnant, and we look forward to her new foal. Mother misses you terribly, but she has stopped crying every night. We would all love to hear from you, so please write us when you are able.*

*I am, and remain, your loyal brother, Harold.*

What a relief to hear mundane news from my family amidst the strange chaos of the last several days. I pictured my sisters around the table griping about the cold, demanding new dresses for spring, and longing for the summer sun to take away the paleness that the long, dark winter had left in their faces. I thought about Mother bustling around the hearth and Father coming in from the cold after a long day of work. But most of all, I thought about Harold, finally growing into a robust young man who could carry hay and water to the horses.

Mother was right to have been so protective of Harold. After his feverish bout of illness when we were young, his health was never quite the same. A year could pass without a problem, but then one day we would chase each other around the barn, and suddenly he would look at me with terrified eyes. His chest would heave, wheezing and whistling sounds escaping his mouth. I would help him inside as he coughed and gasped, and Mother would send me for the doctor. After these attacks subsided, he spent days in bed until he got strong enough to go back to school. There was no way to predict the incidents, and for the first few weeks after an attack, Harold was filled with trepidation. But, after about a month, he lost his fear. He wanted to be treated like a normal boy, and just when he began to feel like one, another attack would hit, knocking him down again and fueling Mother's fears. When he got older, Harold himself was no longer afraid. He refused to let his condition control his life, pleading with Mother and Father to allow him the same freedoms I was given as a young man and to give him the same responsibilities on the farm. When I left home last month, he had not experienced a bout for nearly two years. We all hoped he had outgrown his affliction, but only time would tell.

I folded his letter, blew out the candle, lay back on my pillow, and awoke the next morning in the same position, the letter still held to my chest.

# Chapter 25
## A Dinner Invitation

*Elizabeth Stutsman*

I stayed awake most of the night, sitting on the floor next to Enos's bed to hear his breathing, fighting the impulse to drift off to sleep. He seemed quite comfortable, and every so often my eyelids drooped and I jumped awake. I kept wood in the stove, warming the room to such a temperature that my bodice dampened with perspiration. By morning, Enos stirred and called to me.

"Mama? What are you doing here?"

"Enos. You're awake. I have been here all night. Do you not remember what happened?"

He thought for a moment. "Oh, yes. I was very cold and tired."

"How do you feel today?" I felt his cheeks and forehead.

"I feel just fine, Mama. I'm hungry for breakfast." He began to sit up.

"Really, Enos, you need to rest." I fluffed his pillow so he could lean against it. "It is Sunday, and we have no obligations. I'll ask Ginny to bring our breakfast here today."

"But, Mama..."

"Just rest, son. I'll return right away."

I began to walk toward the kitchen, but as I rounded a corner, I saw Ginny coming down the hall with a tray in her hands.

"Good morning, Mrs. Stutsman," she called. "I thought I might bring you and the boy breakfast."

"How thoughtful of you," I said and stopped to wait for her. We walked back to Enos's room together.

"How is Enos today?" she asked.

"It is strange. It seems as if nothing happened at all," I replied. "His eyes are bright, and he appears full of energy."

We opened Enos's door to find him sitting upright in bed.

"Enos! I told you to rest."

"Mama, I said I feel fine. I am not sick at all."

"Here is your breakfast," said Ginny, placing the tray on the bed before him.

"I am starving!" said Enos, picking up the bread and devouring it as if he had not eaten in days.

"What did I tell you, Ginny? Like nothing happened."

Ginny smiled. "He's a hearty little boy!" She turned and left us alone in the room.

"Enos, Mr. Watson seemed to know you were in danger last evening. Did you see him?" I asked.

"I did, right before I fell in the water. He was running toward me."

"Do you recall what happened next?"

"The next thing I remember, Mama, was waking up

here at the museum."

I was taking a sip of coffee when someone knocked at the door.

"Come in," I said.

It was Arthur. "Good morning," he whispered.

"We're just eating breakfast, Mr. Watson," said Enos.

"Well!" said Arthur. "It appears the young man has fully recovered." He reached over and tousled Enos's hair.

"Good day, Mr. Watson," I said. "I am encouraging him to stay still today. He needs his rest."

"Certainly," said Arthur. "Would you mind if I pulled a chair in from your room and sat awhile?"

"Of course not."

Arthur left for a moment and returned with a wooden chair, which he placed at the foot of Enos's bed.

Enos spoke in between bites of fried ham. "I came looking for you last night, Mr. Watson. I went up and down a few streets, but I couldn't find you."

"Yes," said Arthur. "Enos, do you remember what happened at the river?"

"I thought you might have gone to the river to think," said Enos.

I looked over at Arthur. "Dr. Drake said we are very lucky that Dr. Bell found Enos when he did." I turned back to Enos. "Do you realize you could have died from exposure?"

"Mama, I was perfectly fine."

"Enos! You don't understand. That was far too long a distance for you to travel by yourself after dark in the cold, and the river could have swept you away forever."

Enos glowered. "I am old enough, Mama." His voice rose. "You make no sense. You'll send me away in a wagon with a stranger, but you will not let me go out in the city alone."

My jaw dropped, and Arthur averted his eyes. I tried to stay calm. "Son, you will not speak to me in such a manner. You could have died. You are not an ordinary boy."

"But I am!" he cried. "Leave me alone!" He threw aside the tray and dishes, fell back on the bed, and pulled the covers over his head. "Go away."

Arthur was stunned, but I had grown accustomed to Enos's occasional outbursts. I accepted them as his way of coping with being different.

"Perhaps we should take a stroll," said Arthur. "Give him some time to calm down."

I rose from my chair. "Enos." I placed my hand on the blanket and felt the round curve of his shoulder through the wool. "I'm sorry if I upset you. We are going out for a few moments. Please stay here."

He just huffed and pulled away from my touch.

"Sometimes it is so difficult," I said as we strolled down the hall, morning light coming through the windows.

"I cannot fathom your taking this on alone, Mrs. Stutsman."

"He is a good boy. So smart, so loving. I should have never brought him here. I should have never subjected him to this kind of life." I thought I might cry but did not, which may have appeared strange to Arthur.

"He has such aspirations, such energy, which go beyond the abilities of his physical body," said Arthur. "Mrs. Stutsman… Elizabeth." We stopped walking when we reached the museum's front doors, and Arthur looked me square in the eyes. "I must tell you, I am certain about what happened last evening. I jumped into the water to pull Enos out, and a man appeared. I thought it was Bell coming to help. He reached out his arms, and I lifted Enos into them. And then he shoved me back into the water."

"Mr. Watson—do you realize the gravity of these allegations?"

"Of course. I would not press them if I was not absolutely certain. Bell was the one who carried Enos back, was he not?"

I took a deep breath and began walking again. I thought long and hard.

"Honestly, it was dark, you were cold. Perhaps you are mistaken. You may have fallen in the river yourself. Dr. Bell said he found Enos unconscious in an alley."

"What does the boy remember?"

"Almost nothing. He remembers seeing you, falling in the water, and awaking here," I said. "Dr. Bell has no reason to lie. It could have been someone else."

I could see Arthur thinking hard.

"It looked like Bell, I think. Why would someone help pull Enos out of the river only to leave him lying in an alley?"

"Arthur," I laid my hand on his sleeve. "You had a

difficult night. Dr. Bell was not exactly kind to you in his demonstration. I believe your mind may have been playing tricks on you."

He was quiet for a while and appeared troubled. "Perhaps you are right." He sighed. "Enos may not have lost his balance and fallen off the dock if he would have had crutches. We must find a way to get them. Dr. Drake has already taken his measurements."

"I was stubborn about it for a long time, and now I know. But we have no money. You have no money. We must use everything Enos earns here to live on and to get him to school."

"The crutches will give Enos the independence he needs. As his body grows, he cannot continue dragging himself around with his arms." said Arthur.

Just then Dr. Bell approached from down the corridor. He acted surprised when he saw Arthur and me.

"Good morning," he said, and tipped his hat. "I apologize if I am interrupting."

"Of course not," I said. "Good day, Dr. Bell."

Arthur nodded to him curtly.

"How is the boy?" asked Dr. Bell.

"He is quite fine," I said. "His strength amazes me. He awoke without a sign of yesterday's distress."

"That's wonderful news. May I say hello to him?"

"I know you must be very concerned for him, but Mrs. Stutsman wants him to rest," Arthur blurted.

"It's true. He needs his rest," I said, "But there is no reason why you cannot see him a moment, to wish him well." I threw an annoyed glance at Arthur.

"Thank you, ma'am."

"I'll warn you, however," I continued, "That he is a bit upset right now. He does not want to stay in his room today."

"Why am I not surprised by that?" Dr. Bell quipped.

The three of us walked back toward Enos's room. I opened the door, and saw that Enos had come out from under the blankets and now held a book.

"Enos," I said, as sweetly as possible. "You have another visitor."

He did not put the book down but feigned reading.

"Enos," said Dr. Bell, pushing past me into the room. "How are you feeling?"

Enos looked up briefly, but his eyes quickly returned to the pages of his book.

"Enos," I said, "Dr. Bell asked you a question."

"Fine," he said, not lifting his eyes again.

"Well, I am happy to see you awake and doing well." Dr. Bell turned to me. "I'll be on my way now, Mrs. Stutsman. I have some business to attend to."

"On a Sunday?" I asked.

"Yes. It is something that simply cannot wait, especially if I am to leave town the morning after my next demonstration."

We ducked back into the hall.

"I hear you'll be leaving Tuesday morning?" asked Arthur.

"Yes," said Dr. Bell. He looked in my eyes. "And I'll be sorry to go. I bid you adieu, Mrs. Stutsman," he said.

"Good day, Watson."

Arthur simply grunted.

I immediately went back into Enos's room.

"Enos! You should not have treated Dr. Bell so harshly."

"He interrupted my reading."

"He saved your life and deserves your respect."

"I told him I was feeling fine. There is something I don't like about him."

"He kindly came by to give you his regards. Next time you'll be more considerate."

"All right, Mama." And he just kept reading.

I stepped back into the hall to speak with Arthur.

"How can such a good boy be so bad at times?" I asked.

"Boys will be boys," returned Arthur. "I challenged my parents many times. Now that I do not see them every day, I wish I had been better."

Arthur suddenly turned his face toward me as if he had just remembered something.

"What is it?" I asked.

"With all the excitement I just plain forgot. Dorfoy asked me to deliver a letter to Mr. Longworth yesterday evening."

"You forgot to deliver it?"

"Oh, no. I visited his house just before Dr. Bell's demonstration."

"Do you mean Nicholas Longworth who lives in the grand home on Pike Street? You set foot in his house?"

"Yes! The home is marvelous indeed. Mr. Longworth is a bit peculiar but very kind. He extended a dinner invitation to us. He wants to meet Enos. Mr. Powers and his wife will be there as well."

"How wonderful! When?"

"Dinner is to be this very evening."

"Oh, how disappointing! Enos simply cannot leave his bed."

"Are you sure, Mrs. Stutsman? What if he rests all day?"

"I will have to consider it."

"If he rides in Mr. Dorfoy's carriage? Please think about it. Enos will love to see the house. It would lift his spirits tremendously. The place is filled with mammoth paintings and fireplaces so large you could stand in them."

"I said I would consider it. Really, Mr. Watson, you sound like a child yourself!"

Arthur collected himself. "My apologies. Mr. Longworth is very good company. He is a very interesting character, and I believe you will enjoy yourself as much as Enos."

"Let us see how Enos feels this afternoon. If he is not up to it, I will simply stay here with him, and the rest of you may go."

"I would hate to leave the two of you behind," Arthur said softly.

# Chapter 26
# The Crutches

*Arthur Watson*

I was filled with confusion over the incident at the river. It began to feel like a dream that faded slowly in the waking hours. I was certain of what had happened, yet I struggled for a clear picture of the man's face in my mind. Perhaps I had been mistaken. Dr. Bell was well-respected and would know that I would tell everyone the truth unless he thought he had left me there to drown. As much as the man seemed to hate me, I had no evidence to prove he was there.

All this aside, I had never felt so thrilled as when I saw Enos sitting up in bed eating his breakfast. Just the evening before, he had faced death in the frigid waters of the Ohio, and I thought he was lost forever in the arms of that shadowy man. The boy was remarkably brave to venture out on his own to search for me. I was wallowing in my own doubts and fears, worrying about what others thought of me, as Enos risked death to find me! I thought I had rescued him: first from the fight on that fateful evening when I met him and now from the icy water. But I was wrong. I hadn't rescued him at all. When I saw him awake and strong this morning, I realized that this boy had saved *me*.

I wanted to repay him, but I had nothing to give. I realized now that I wanted to take care of him and Elizabeth for the rest of their lives, but Elizabeth would never take me seriously, not after my ridiculous mistakes. I worked for a man who could not even pay me. I drank and insulted her choice of company. I was berated in public for my weak character. Now, I had led her son out into the forbidding winter streets of Cincinnati, and he had barely survived. Worst of all, she believed that another man saved his life. All I could do was to begin with something small, a token of how much I cared for Enos, of how I wanted to change their lives. I decided to pay another visit to Dr. Drake. Elizabeth was as stubborn as they came, but I knew once she saw Enos using his crutches, she'd accept my help.

I felt strange calling on the doctor on a Sunday. I was sure he spent the day with his family, but the urgency of the matter propelled me on. I waited until afternoon when I hoped his church responsibilities would be completed. The day was mild for February, so I left my coat open and the breeze blew it out on either side like a kite. When I reached the doctor's office, I knocked. His assistant answered.

"I'm sorry, but the doctor left just a few minutes ago," he said.

"Do you know when he will return?" I asked.

"I am not sure. Another gentleman accompanied him."

"Thank you." I said, handing him my card. "Please tell him I called."

"Certainly, sir. Good day to you."

"Good day." I tipped my hat and turned back toward the street.

I walked back to the museum, deciding to put these last few daunting days behind me and focus on making Enos and Elizabeth permanent fixtures in my life. I paused before the window of a fancy store to look at a small tortoiseshell comb. After I paid for Enos's crutches and saved some more money, I would come back to buy it for Elizabeth. I looked at the sky and let the sun warm my face. I closed my eyes and took a deep breath, feeling quite certain of my destiny. Continuing on, I greeted everyone who passed me, and each returned a kind word. When I arrived at the museum, I held the door open for a young woman whose husband had dropped her and her small son at the door in their carriage. I walked in behind them and heard her say to the boy, "Let's wait right here for your father." I would have to find another time to speak with the doctor again soon, but at least now I knew my plan.

It was late afternoon, and several families browsed around the museum. Dorfoy promoted Sunday as a family day, he had told me, because he closed early and did not present evening performances. Sunday was the only day most men did not work and provided the only hours they could spend with their children. While most still chose to spend those hours at home observing the

Sabbath, many sought out activities on which to spend their small earnings, and the museum was after all only a quarter, with children free on Sundays. I turned down the corridor. As I approached the Stutsmans' rooms, I heard lilting voices and the sound of a few people clapping. The door was slightly ajar so I peered inside. They remained oblivious to my presence.

"This is wonderful. Absolutely wonderful!" exclaimed Elizabeth, her back to the doorway.

"They will take some getting used to, but you realize this will change his life forever," said a man with a familiar deep voice. "I cannot stay, because I promised my family I would spend the day with them," he continued, "but you keep practicing, Enos."

"We are so grateful," said Elizabeth.

"Yes, thank you," echoed Enos.

"Good day to you both," the man said, "and to you, Dr. Bell."

"Likewise," I heard Bell say.

Just as the door opened, I placed the man's voice. And now his face appeared, looking pleased. It was Dr. Drake.

"Mr. Watson. You startled me." As Dr. Drake came out into the hall, I saw what had been happening in the room. Enos held himself up on a pair of small crutches, his face beaming. I could do nothing but stare at him. The crutches fit underneath his arms, extending them several inches. Rather than bent forward, as was his usual posture, he held his body upright. He appeared confident and strong.

"Aren't you thrilled, Mr. Watson?" asked Dr. Drake.

"It is as you wished."

"Why, yes, but..."

"After last night, I knew he needed them right away, so I brought them by this morning. I haven't time to explain now," said the doctor, "but I shall see you soon and tell you the entire story."

"Thank you," I said.

"You need not thank me," said the doctor. "Good day Mr. Watson."

"Good day, doctor."

He hurried down the hall, and I just stood there watching him until he rounded the corner and was out of sight.

"Mr. Watson!" called Enos. "Come see."

I shook my head to ground my thoughts as I walked into his room. "Of course, Enos."

"Good day, Mr. Watson," said Elizabeth, turning to me. "Isn't this amazing?"

I was right. The minute Elizabeth saw Enos using the crutches, all worries about taking charity fell away. Her eyes sparkled as she looked proudly at her son. She was the most beautiful I had ever seen her.

"Good day, Watson," said Dr. Bell, rising from his chair.

"Greetings, Dr. Bell," I said, bowing to him.

I turned immediately back toward Enos, crouching down to speak with him.

"How do they feel?" I asked.

"A little funny, but look!" He used the crutches to propel his body easily onto the bed, then back down

204| TAMERA LENZ MUENTE

again. He turned around and moved quickly back to me.

"You will be racing around in no time," I said.

"Mama, can I go out and practice in the hallway?"

"Certainly, Enos. But please do not go far. The doctor said it will take some time for you to build up your endurance, as you are still recovering from last night."

Enos moved past me quickly and out into the corridor.

"Isn't this exciting?" asked Elizabeth again.

"Yes, of course, but how?"

"Dr. Drake and Dr. Bell came in just a short time ago and presented them to Enos."

I must have looked like a bewildered dog that had just been kicked.

Bell interrupted. "If you mean how were they paid for, I don't want to take all the credit, because it was really the dear doctor, but..."

Elizabeth spun around. "You paid for them?"

"Well, as I said," continued Bell calmly, "I don't want to take credit, but I did speak with the doctor, and he said the only thing standing in the way of Enos getting the crutches was a lack of financing. I thought, what a terrible shame that money should stand in the way of the boy's freedom."

The room was silent. I was preparing for one of Elizabeth's proud speeches about charity, but instead she rushed over to Bell and threw her arms around him.

"How can I ever thank you enough?" she exclaimed, her face pink as she quickly withdrew her embrace. "Beg pardon, Dr. Bell. I was overcome and could not control myself." She patted down the folds of her skirt and backed away.

"There is no reason to show me such gratitude. It was nothing," he replied.

I watched them look at each other and could not believe what I was seeing and hearing. Elizabeth had rejected my idea just days ago, and now she was literally throwing herself at Bell.

"What's the matter, Mr. Watson?" asked Bell, noticing my state of shock.

I could think of nothing to say except, "Mrs. Stutsman, I thought you wanted Enos to rest today after his ordeal last evening."

"How can you be negative at a time like this? This is what you wanted, isn't it?" She scowled. "Please be happy for us."

Of course I was overjoyed for them, but I could not summon the words to tell her. I simply looked at Elizabeth, then down at the floor, then slowly turned and left the room.

"Does the invitation to Mr. Longworth's still stand for this evening?" she called after me, but I did not turn around.

Enos ambled down the hall, his new crutches like extensions of his own arms. Already he moved faster and with more ease. When he reached the end of the corridor, he picked up his right crutch, crossed it in front of his body, and placed it carefully next to the left crutch. He then moved the left crutch slightly behind his body and turned slowly. When he faced me, I saw him smiling wider than I had ever witnessed. This pleased me, but, oh, how I ached that I was not the one to give him, and likewise his mother, such joy.

# Chapter 27
## Dinner with
## Mr. Nicholas Longworth

*Elizabeth Stutsman*

Enos and I went to see Mr. Dorfoy in his office. I had never seen my son look so happy, nor had I seen him move around so rapidly. Now I would have to worry about keeping up with him. Mr. Dorfoy answered the door after just one knock.

"Greetings, Mrs. Stutsman," he said in his usual polite voice.

"Good day, Mr. Dorfoy," I replied. "I have a surprise for you."

Enos poked his head into the doorway. "Look, Mr. Dorfoy!" He moved in next to me and lifted one crutch high in the air.

"Enos—don't show off," I scolded.

"My heavens!" Mr. Dorfoy exclaimed. "What is this?"

"Dr. Drake brought me crutches this morning," answered Enos.

"Well, I'll be. The good doctor is a very generous man."

"I believe he had the assistance of Dr. Bell," I said.

"Very interesting. Damien Bell has taken quite an

interest in you and your son, Mrs. Stutsman."

I felt heat rise in my cheeks. "He was just being kind."

"Well, whatever it was, I am just happy it was I who introduced the two of you," Mr. Dorfoy beamed.

"Come out in the hall and see how they work," said Enos.

Mr. Dorfoy followed Enos out of the room, and the boy began pacing back and forth with his crutches.

"That is wonderful, absolutely stupendous, Enos!"

Then, Mr. Dorfoy pulled me by the elbow back into his office.

"You realize, Mrs. Stutsman, that we had an agreement when you came here."

I was not sure what he meant, but I nonetheless answered that of course I understood.

"So you know what I am getting at?"

I just looked at him, trying to read his expression, which now appeared stern.

"Enos cannot use those crutches when on stage. The effect is entirely uninteresting. They will ruin the show."

My mouth dropped open, but I quickly regained my composure. I did not want to appear ungrateful to Mr. Dorfoy.

"Why, certainly, Mr. Dorfoy. I never thought otherwise." I did not know how I would tell Enos, but for now I did not want to offend the man who was keeping us out of the poorhouse.

"Very good. As long as we are clear. Now, what is this about a dinner invitation to Mr. Longworth's this very evening?"

I sighed and walked out of Mr. Dorfoy's office without answering him.

I had thought it important for Enos to rest today, but I had never seen him in such high spirits. I did not have the heart to tell him we could not join the rest of the party for dinner. After a few turns about the grand hall of the museum to clear my mind, I went to Enos's room and found him there, reading.

"Hello, Mama. I am resting like you asked."

"Thank you, Enos, for obeying me."

"Now, can I go practice walking with my crutches again?"

"Oh, you'll get plenty of practice in just a short while. We've been invited to dinner this evening."

"With Dr. Bell?" he asked, sounding disappointed.

"No. I did ask him to join us, but he politely declined. We will have dinner with Mr. Nicholas Longworth, a wealthy and generous gentleman who is Mr. Dorfoy's close associate."

"It sounds dull." He kept reading.

"Enos!" I snatched the book away from him and closed it. He frowned. "He is also a very good friend of Mr. Powers, who will be there as well."

"Mr. Powers?" He perked up. "Will Mr. Watson be there, too?"

"Yes."

Enos sprung out of bed. "Well, I should get cleaned up then, shouldn't I Mama?"

"You certainly should. Put on your best shirt and the

new breeches I just finished for you. We will be riding in Mr. Dorfoy's carriage. It will be ready at seven o'clock."

"Can I bring the crutches?"

I smiled. "Yes, Enos. Absolutely." I ducked out of his room and into mine to begin to prepare for dinner.

I sat on my bed in disgust. I would have to wear the blue dress I had planned to wear to supper after Dr. Bell's performance. But cotton! It would be so wonderful to wear silk to a formal dinner at the grand house. It was the best gown I owned, however. Unfortunately, I had not the time to attach the new lace I had been saving for its bodice. I would complete that Monday to freshen the dress before the doctor's second performance that evening. At least it was a good dress, well-made and lovely, and would do for tonight.

It was near seven o'clock, so I went to Enos's room to make sure he would be ready. There he was, in his best white shirt and new woolen breeches, standing tall with his crutches. He had smoothed his hair back to one side and smiled widely.

"Well, don't you look quite the little gentleman?"

"I want to make a good impression on Mr. Longworth. I will be delighted to see Mr. Powers again. He is a very nice man."

I held the door open so Enos could come into the hallway. It was as if he had used the crutches since birth. He moved smoothly and quickly beside me down the corridor. We arrived at the museum's entrance hall to meet Mr. Dorfoy and Arthur, who were already waiting.

Arthur bowed and greeted us. "You look lovely this evening, Mrs. Stutsman. And, Enos, you look to be getting along very well with your new crutches. I am delighted you are feeling well enough to join us."

"I have been telling Mama all day that I am just fine."

"Well, it is our mothers' responsibility to make sure we are safe and healthy," Arthur replied. "Your mother would never forgive herself if you had a recurrence of the terrible state you were in last evening."

Thomas opened the doors for us, signaling that the carriage was ready. I walked out with Mr. Dorfoy taking my arm. Enos and Arthur followed behind, chatting away.

"Where is Mr. Powers?" asked Enos.

"He and his wife will meet us there," Arthur replied.

"Is Mr. Longworth's house very big?"

"I have been inside just once, and yes, it is grand and filled with wonderful furniture, paintings, and sculptures."

"Is he a kind gentleman?"

"I have met him only once, Enos, but I think you will find him very gracious indeed."

Thomas helped me up into the carriage, and Mr. Dorfoy followed. Then, Arthur lifted Enos inside and climbed in beside him.

"Thomas," called Mr. Dorfoy, "Take the long way around. Let us show the boy some of the city."

It was already dark, but the full moon reflected off the snow, allowing us to see some of our surroundings. Thomas drove to the public landing, where two steamboats were docked. Enos looked out the carriage window gleefully.

"There is the river, Mama," he said. The awful Ohio had almost claimed my son, yet it appeared quite beautiful as moonlight bounced off its surface, and floating chunks of ice sparkled as they bobbed up and down.

Finally, Thomas pulled the horses up in front of Mr. Longworth's home. "There is Belmont, the most beautiful house in Cincinnati," said Mr. Dorfoy.

I could hardly believe we had been invited to such a place. The house rose up before us like a Greek temple. I felt my pulse rise. Mr. Dorfoy stepped out of the carriage and offered me his hand. Arthur climbed out and helped Enos down.

"This is Mr. Longworth's house?" asked Enos. "It looks like a palace."

"Yes," I replied. "This is Mr. Longworth's home. I expect you to be on your best behavior."

Enos's eyes stared up in wonder as we ascended the stairs up to the front door. We stepped between the columns that flanked the front porch, and Mr. Dorfoy grasped the great brass doorknocker and tapped it. Just a few seconds later, the door creaked open, and a man with rumpled hair and baggy clothes answered.

"Nicholas, my dear friend!" exclaimed Mr. Dorfoy.

I was truly surprised to hear that this nondescript man was the great Mr. Longworth.

"So wonderful to see you, Joseph! It has been a long winter, has it not?"

"Indeed."

"Please, come in." Mr. Longworth stepped aside to allow us to walk into the foyer. "I am thrilled you all could come. As I told Mr. Watson the other evening, my family is away, and I am terribly lonely in this big house."

My nervousness melted in this man's presence. He was gracious, unassuming, and welcoming. He stretched out his hand toward Enos.

"Hello, young man," he said. "You must be Enos."

Enos took his hand. "Yes, sir. I'm very pleased to meet you, Mr. Longworth."

Once Mr. Dorfoy completed the formal introductions, Mr. Longworth invited us inside the parlor. Mr. Powers was already inside, and stood to cordially greet us.

"You already know Mr. Powers," said Mr. Longworth.

"I have not yet had the pleasure," I said, curtsying.

"You have an incredible son there, Mrs. Stutsman," he said.

"Thank you, Mr. Powers. He admires you a great deal."

"Mr. Powers," said Enos. "Have you finished the wax figure you were working on?"

"Why, yes, Enos, and I'm on to the next one already."

"Is Mr. Dorfoy keeping you so busy that you'll not have time to begin my portrait?" asked Mr. Longworth.

"Oh, for heaven's sake, Nicholas," cried Mr. Dorfoy. "The public requires change to keep their attention. He'll have time, he'll have time."

The three men laughed, and we all moved to the parlor. The furniture was very fine, upholstered in satin and velvet. I looked over at Enos, who glanced around in awe.

"Mama, look at this painting." He gestured toward a landscape that hung over one of the sofas. "It is so lifelike."

"It is very lovely."

"Do you like art?" Mr. Longworth asked Enos.

"I have not seen much of it, Mr. Longworth. It looks wonderful, but I believe I prefer stories."

"You do know that the greatest of paintings tell stories, don't you?"

"I think I shall like that kind of art best."

"Why don't you come with me? Mrs. Stutsman, you may join us as well. Gentlemen, we will return shortly." Mr. Longworth led Enos and me out of the parlor, around the corner, and into a massive room hung with two large chandeliers. Windows decorated with heavy satin curtains lined one side of the room.

"If it was daylight, from these windows we could look over my garden all the way to my vineyards," he said.

Enos and I looked up and around the room. The walls were covered with pictures. At one end was a large painting with figures bigger than life. Mr. Longworth gestured toward it.

"This is what I wanted you to see," said Mr. Longworth.

We moved closer until we stood before the huge canvas that stretched nearly to the ceiling.

"It's so big," exclaimed Enos. "And the people appear alive! Is he a king? What is wrong with her?" He pointed to a pale young woman in white who looked entranced, her eyes vacant and staring.

"You have heard of the great William Shakespeare, yes?"

"Of course," replied Enos, "but Mama won't let me read his plays. She says I am too young. But I know I am smart enough." He shot me an irritated glance.

"Enos," I replied, "it is not about being smart enough."

"Your mother is probably right," said Mr. Longworth. "Shakespeare wrote about such complicated human drama, your young mind may have a difficult time grasping it. Do not worry. It will be worth the wait."

"Is that Mr. Shakespeare sitting in the throne?" asked Enos.

"My dear boy," Mr. Longworth chuckled. "This is a part of a story written by Shakespeare. The painter Benjamin West, an American who lived in London, set out to paint every act of Shakespeare's *Hamlet* but only finished a few before they had to be sold."

"How unfortunate," I said.

"They were purchased by an American, the man who had made a fortune with his invention of the steam-powered boat. When I heard the Fulton estate was up for sale, I knew I had to have this painting. His heirs sent it down the river on a flatboat, and it arrived here safely, as if it were a miracle."

"You said it told a story," said Enos.

Mr. Longworth crouched down beside Enos so his eyes were level with the boy's.

"Well, let's see. The couple seated on the right, as I am

sure you have guessed by now, are the king and queen. But, he is not the real king—he murdered the real king, who was his brother, so he could steal the throne."

"Is that why the queen looks down? Is she thinking about her dead husband?" asked Enos.

"How very observant of you. I believe she also feels guilty, because she suspects the murder."

"What is the matter with that girl?"

"Poor Ophelia. Hamlet, the queen's son, who is not in this picture, is pretending to be insane in order to reveal the truth about his uncle's plot. Ophelia and Hamlet were in love, but even Ophelia believes that Hamlet has lost his mind. As part of his scheme, Hamlet accidentally murders Ophelia's father, and she goes insane. In the picture, her brother, Laertes, presents her to the king and queen. Laertes will later avenge his sister by killing Hamlet with a poisoned sword."

"What a terrible, tragic tale," I said.

"What a terrific story!" exclaimed Enos. Mr. Longworth laughed.

"Notice the details that tell the story in the painting. Ophelia is dropping flowers to the ground, reminding us of her famous lines in the play, '...rosemary, that's for remembrance; pray, love, remember: and there is pansies. That's for thoughts."

"For thoughts," I said. When Jacob died, I had presented his mother with a posy of pansies. I felt a pang in my heart.

Ophelia's vacant stare was quite startling, and the graceful gestures of her long, pale arms beautiful and sad.

The three of us stood there for what felt like a long while, silently studying the picture.

Mr. Longworth broke the reverie. "I don't know about you, but I am feeling exceedingly famished. Shall we?" He offered his elbow to me, and I hooked my arm in his.

"Yes. I am starving!" said Enos. And off he went.

"Your son has the glimmer of great intelligence in his eyes, Mrs. Stutsman."

The two of us strolled slowly down the hall, as I took in the luxurious surroundings.

"Why, thank you. I have tried to teach him well."

"What I sense is beyond education," continued Mr. Longworth. "I can see he possesses the essence of what makes a man great. Perhaps his physical shortcomings have strengthened his perseverance."

"I do think there is truth to that, Mr. Longworth. I've never been able to slow him down."

Mr. Longworth smiled and patted my hand, and we rounded the corner into the parlor. Enos had already thrust himself down on the sofa next to Mr. Powers, who was gesturing wildly with his hands while Arthur and Mr. Dorfoy laughed heartily. I regretted interrupting the gay scene.

"Might we take this party to the dining room?" asked Mr. Longworth.

The gentlemen rose, and Mr. Powers helped Enos down from the sofa.

"He is getting on wonderfully with those crutches," said the sculptor.

"Yes," I replied. "He is now quicker than ever."

Our party made its way down the hall. Upon entering the dining room, I could see a long mahogany table lit with three candelabra and set with fine silver. Two servants stood at the far end of the room and bowed slightly as we entered. I had never seen such an elegant scene. Laid out on the table were six place settings of fine china. Mr. Longworth pulled out my chair and bade me to sit down. Once I was seated, the rest of our party took their seats. I looked at the delicate plates before me. They were bone-white, edged with tangerine and gold. In the center were two quail arranged in ribbons of marsh grass. A crystal glass on a long stem stood to the left of my plate, catching the light from the flickering candles. To the right, I saw a small bowl filled with water. As I struggled to decide its purpose, I glanced over to see Mr. Dorfoy placing his fingers in the bowl. A servant quickly arrived at his side with a clean white towel on which he dried his hands. I looked at Enos, then over to Mr. Longworth, who was now performing the finger cleaning, then back at Enos, who glanced knowingly at me, then fluttered his fingers in the water. I did the same as the servant brought us a towel.

The other servant, a tall, slender dark-skinned man, presented a reddish brown bottle.

"French wine," said Mr. Longworth.

"You need not pour this on our account," returned Mr. Dorfoy.

"My wine is pleasing," Mr. Longworth continued, "but this is a special occasion."

The servant began to make his way round the table, filling our crystal glasses with the deep claret liquid. I thought about placing my hand over the glass but then thought again. Such a gesture might be deemed ungrateful in such refined company. I would be gracious and forego my temperance just this one night. After all, wine was a civilized drink, hardly the same as whiskey.

Mr. Longworth lifted his glass. "To my new friends!" Everyone lifted theirs, and sipped the wine. I did the same. The liquid warmed my mouth with the flavor of smoky wood and cherries and burned as it went down. I felt it settle like a lump in my stomach.

Enos leaned over. "Mama," he whispered, "I don't very much care for this." He blinked his eyes toward his wine.

"Don't fret, my dear," I said quietly. "Just don't drink it, then." He sat back in his chair, looking very relieved.

Now a young woman appeared with a crock. She ladled clear broth into another small bowl at each of our place settings. The boullion smelled wonderful, of vegetables and spices. Once everyone had been served, I nodded at Enos, and we both picked up our spoons. It was delicious.

The servant who had brought around the towels now returned with a small cart, on which sat a steaming roast. He cut into it with a long knife, revealing the rosy middle and letting clear pink juices flow onto the platter. Only on the most important occasions did we eat roast beef, and not since Jacob had passed. The smell of it literally made my mouth water. The servant placed a thin slice on my plate, then one on Enos's. The young maid followed, spooning on a generous portion of root vegetables flavored with parsley. Once the eating began, so did the conversation. The six of us exchanged pleasantries, and Mr. Longworth kept me enthralled with such wonderful stories. Mr. Dorfoy, too, shared fantastic tales from his museum that made us all gasp and laugh. It was in the middle of one such story that I felt Arthur's eyes upon me from across the table. I felt my face go warm, and I looked down at my plate of food. I picked up my wine glass and took a sip, turning in the direction of Mr. Powers.

"Mr. Powers," I began, "I am disappointed that your wife could not join us this evening."

"So am I, Mrs. Stutsman. I feel the two of you would get on quite well," he replied. "She was looking very pale and tired, so I bade her to stay home. I am sure you know first-hand the exhaustion that can plague a woman."

I did not quite know what to say, and the exchange fell flat. For a few moments, the room was quiet. Then, Arthur began to tell the story of how he had met Enos. I was relieved for the change of subject and glanced in his direction. His eyes met mine, and this time I did not turn away.

# Chapter 28
## A Lovely Evening

*Arthur Watson*

**M**r. Longworth saw us to our carriage himself. The evening had confirmed that he was a very gracious gentleman, indeed.

"Good evening, dear friends!" he called, waving as our carriage pulled away.

It was late, and all four of us were tired. Enos slumped against his mother's side, dozing off as the carriage bounced back toward the museum. Mr. Dorfoy, who sat next to me, looked out the small window into the darkness. Elizabeth sat directly across from me, and I took a deep breath, trying to pretend I did not notice that our knees almost touched.

Elizabeth broke the silence. "What a lovely evening," she said. "I could not have imagined such a wonderful host."

"Mr. Longworth is a great and loyal man," returned Dorfoy. "He is perhaps the most generous man in Cincinnati."

Elizabeth looked at me and smiled, more beautiful than ever. I had seen her in nothing but black since our first meeting, and the blue dress she wore tonight enlivened her face and brought out the golden highlights of her hair. I returned her gaze, and she quickly turned her eyes out the window. The carriage rattled on and soon alighted at the museum's entrance. I climbed out of the carriage first and helped the half-asleep boy from his seat.

"Here, let me carry you, Enos," I said. I picked him up, and he immediately fell asleep again on my shoulder.

"The past two days have been exhausting for him" said Elizabeth as she handed Enos's crutches down to Dorfoy, who held them in one hand as he helped her down.

"I dare say he will be hard to keep up with now that he has those crutches," I replied as we went inside.

"Mrs. Stutsman, might I remind you of our conversation earlier today," said Dorfoy. I looked over at Elizabeth, and her eyes seemed troubled.

"Of course, Mr. Dorfoy," she replied. "Mr. Watson, I trust you will help me get Enos to his room?"

"Why, yes, of course."

"Good night, then, Mr. Dorfoy." She took the crutches from him.

"Good night to you both."

"Of what was he speaking?" I asked her after Dorfoy was far enough away not to hear.

"It was nothing."

"It obviously upset you."

She opened the door to Enos's room, and I carried him inside and laid him on his bed. She pulled his blankets up to his chin. "Not in here," she whispered, and we went back into the hallway.

Elizabeth began to pace a short path the width of her doorway.

"What is it?" I asked again.

"Mr. Dorfoy does not want Enos to use his crutches on stage."

I could hardly fathom the man's cruelty. "That is hardly fair!" I exclaimed.

"Shhh," protested Elizabeth. "Enos does not know yet."

"I cannot believe his insensitivity."

She stopped and thought a moment. "Strangely, I understand. He makes his livelihood from showing monstrosities. Enos appears more... human if he walks upright."

"Mrs. Stutsman!" I scolded.

She shook her head. "Of course, I did not mean that. He is my son for God's sake. But people expect to see someone who is more like an animal. Part of our livelihood depends on that as well."

I could hardly believe she was saying this. "Have you seen any money from Dorfoy? Has he paid you yet?"

"Well, no, but..."

"He has not paid me either."

"Keep your voice down," she said again. "Come in here." She opened the door to her room.

The impropriety of being in her room so late at night crossed my mind, and it surely entered hers as well. We went inside nevertheless.

"Sit," she said as she lit a lamp. "I do not know how to make you understand. We have no other choice." Her eyes began to glisten.

"But I do understand," I said in earnest.

"Mr. Watson. You are young and see a world full of possibilities."

"I am not so much younger than you," I protested.

"Not in age, of course," she replied. "But you do not know the whole of my experience."

"But I could understand. Trust me, Elizabeth," I pleaded. "Unburden yourself. Tell me everything."

"I cannot." Her brow furrowed deeper than I had ever seen it.

"Elizabeth," I said, leaning toward her and looking into her eyes. "The past does not matter to me. What matters is that we were brought together here, now. I want to take you from here, I want to give you and Enos a happy life."

"Please! Arthur, stop." She stood up and walked to the other corner of the room. Even with her voice full of distress, the sound of my name falling from her lips thrilled me.

"But, Elizabeth."

"Be realistic, Arthur." Her voice sounded almost cruel now. "We have just met. You have no money. No occupation. I must think of my son."

"Above all else, I am thinking of Enos," I replied.

She returned to her chair and sat down, her face turned away from me. "You are a man, Arthur."

I tried to decipher this statement as she continued.

"You have no limits. You could walk out of the museum in the morning and find a way to earn a living.

You could find a place to live and have money for food to eat. But it will take time. Do you see?"

I still did not, and she saw my confusion.

"I have had no choice but to rely on men. I cannot make money of my own. I can scarcely walk on the street alone without my propriety being questioned. They will take him from me."

I thought hard about who she meant. The women from the children's home who saw Enos soon after he arrived? Or showmen like Dorfoy, who would prey on his condition to their own ends?

"Then rely on me, Elizabeth."

"I am running out of time."

"I will work hard. I can leave tomorrow and find better work."

"Arthur," she interrupted.

I stopped and looked at her, but still she would not look me in the eye.

"Enos and I are leaving with Dr. Bell the day after tomorrow."

I sat, stunned, not sure if I had heard her correctly. "I beg your pardon?" My stomach grew sick.

"Dr. Bell has offered to help us, but we must leave with him on Tuesday."

Heat rose in my cheeks, and my breath grew heavy.

"Elizabeth. You cannot mean to leave with that swindler!"

"He is no swindler, and I do mean to. It is our last chance. Dr. Bell will not return to this region for some time." Her voice was quivering now.

"Does Mr. Dorfoy know?"

"Of course not. No one knows. I must tell him the news myself tomorrow."

We sat quietly for what seemed an eternity. A log crackled in the stove. Elizabeth shifted in her chair, looking down at her hands. Finally, I rose to leave.

"Arthur, we cannot go back to where we came from. We cannot stay here forever. My son must not live his entire life as a curiosity."

"At least I understand your last point," I said. With my head swimming, I nearly stumbled from the room.

My sleep that night was filled with a fitful dream that played over and over in my mind's eye. Enos stood alone at the end of a long hallway, his crutches propping him up under his arms. He leaned into the left crutch to wave with his right hand. A soft light floating with dust motes filled the space between us as I called his name. I walked slowly toward him, and when I was halfway there, a red velvet curtain fell in front of him. My pace lifted to a run, and when I reached the curtain and pulled it aside, Enos was gone. I awoke with my heart pounding. I must have pulled aside that curtain a hundred times, with every result the same. I thought of the empty space behind it as I lay awake in the darkness of my room, and my whole body ached.

# Chapter 29
## Dr. Bell's Intentions

*Arthur Watson*

The grand hall looked as it always did. Elizabeth was already there, sitting in the same chair, her needlework in her lap as usual. She was not stitching, however, but looking wistfully at Enos, who was on the stage. To my surprise, he was walking from one end to the other with his crutches.

"Good Morning, Mr. Watson!" he called.

This jolted Elizabeth from her reverie, and she turned her head to me.

"Good morning, Mrs. Stutsman." I nodded my head toward the stage. "Did you convince Mr. Dorfoy otherwise?"

"No," she sighed.

"Well, I guess it won't make much difference anyway."

She looked at me and cocked her head, her eyebrows furrowed, showing her confusion without saying a word.

"Given this is his last day here, of course."

"Of course," she replied. "Will you tell him? I just cannot seem to find the right words."

"You want me to tell Enos you are leaving? Please do not ask this of me," I pleaded.

"Not that," she whispered. "Not that. I shall be the one to share that news with him. I am speaking of Mr. Dorfoy's prohibition of his crutches during display hours."

"My apologies." I thought for a moment. "Yes. I believe I can handle that."

I walked over to the stage. Enos was thoroughly proficient with the crutches. His new posture changed his whole countenance. He now held his head erect, and his face glowed with excitement.

"I cannot wait until the weather is warmer so I can play outside with these!" he exclaimed.

"That will be wonderful," I replied, sitting down on the edge of the stage. "Enos, come sit with me a moment."

He looked puzzled but came over. Sitting, I could see, was still a bit awkward for him with his new form of transportation. He swung his body between the crutches, then plopped down on the stage.

"I must practice that," he said.

"You are doing very well," I said, tousling his hair.

"What is it, Mr. Watson?" He was a perceptive child.

"Enos," I said, clearing my throat. "Do you think you could do without the crutches just for this one day?"

"But why?"

"You see, Mr. Dorfoy is so pleased with them, he wishes to unveil them in a special demonstration to the public."

"Oh?"

"He wants to educate people about how they work,

and how they will make your life much easier."

"That is very nice of Mr. Dorfoy," he replied.

"I could bring you a book to read, as you usually do anyway."

"That would be perfect." The boy smiled. "Mama has one I just started." The crutches lay on the stage next to him, and he pushed them in my direction.

"Thank you, Enos." I picked up the crutches and took them back to Elizabeth.

"Is all that true?" she asked.

"I have an entire day to make it so," I replied.

She studied my face. "I admit you do have a way with him."

"With Dorfoy?"

"No!" Elizabeth laughed, small dimples showing in her cheeks. As she giggled, she obscured her face with her hand. Not thinking, I took it in mine and lowered it away from her mouth.

"Do not hide your lovely smile," I said.

She suddenly looked grave. "Please, Mr. Watson."

I let go of her hand and it dropped into her lap. "Must you go through with it, Elizabeth?"

"I feel I must. Let's not speak of it any longer."

I could not hold back.

"He's a scoundrel! Enos does not even like him, and the boy is fond of everyone. I do not trust him, and I certainly would not trust him with Enos in his charge."

"You know him so well?"

"You saw how he treated me, Elizabeth."

"It is not Dr. Bell's fault that your reading did not go

as you had wished. He is perfectly agreeable. Enos will learn to like him with time. He helped Enos get his crutches."

This statement perturbed me beyond anything else. My face grew hot, and I stood up. Stifling my anger, I bid her good day. "I must report to Mr. Dorfoy for today's assignment."

As I walked away, I turned over every possible scenario in my mind. I could not let them go easily. I must find a way to convince her. I could not let her marry Bell.

I already knew that Dorfoy would have me preparing for Bell's demonstration all afternoon. Rather than reporting for duty, however, my legs almost involuntarily propelled me to the door, out into the street, and toward Dr. Drake's office. He certainly knew something of Dr. Bell's reputation before he arrived here.

The same young man answered Dr. Drake's door. "Good morning, Mr. Watson." I had visited the office so many times in the past few days that he now knew me by name.

"Good morning."

"Looking for Dr. Drake?" he asked.

I nodded.

"He is with a patient right now, but he should be finished momentarily. You may wait if you wish."

I sat in one of the chairs near the fire, going over my questions in my head. I did not want to offend Dr. Drake by inquiring about his new friend, so I must proceed carefully. A few moments went by before a woman in a long maroon cape passed me.

"Good day, Mrs. Thompson," the young man called, and she disappeared out the door. "Dr. Drake can see you now."

I walked toward his office door, which was open.

"Greetings, Mr. Watson," called the doctor in his typically cheerful voice. "Won't you come in?"

I entered and sat in the chair across from him. I looked over his desk into his intense eyes.

"How can I be of service today? Are Mrs. Stutsman and her son well?"

"Yes, I believe so."

"And I trust you are well?"

In reality, I did not feel well at all. "Certainly, Dr. Drake. I have come on another matter."

"What is it?"

"How well do you know Dr. Bell?" I was relieved to have asked the question.

"Not very. I have read of his work and find it intriguing, albeit not entirely in line with medical science. Why do you ask?"

"There have been a few people around the museum asking about him. I would like to be able to answer their questions."

"Why not ask him for a bit of biography?"

"I could, doctor, but I have not seen him since yesterday morning. I believe he has been attending to business before he leaves town tomorrow."

"I'm sure of it. He does not come to this part of the

country often."

"So he has said. Now, back to his reputation, if we may."

"Of course. He is perhaps the foremost practitioner of phrenology in the region. From what I could see the other evening, he is also quite the showman."

"That's exactly what I thought," I said.

"There is nothing wrong with being theatrical," the doctor continued, "if research and knowledge form the heart of your material. I am not sure this is true of Dr. Bell, but he is charming and means well."

Perhaps I had judged him poorly. "He does seem generous. Why do you suppose he paid you for Enos's crutches?"

The doctor looked puzzled. "The crutches? Why, Dr. Bell did not pay for them."

"He led us to believe that."

"I am quite certain. The patron wished to remain anonymous."

I thought back to our conversation in Enos's room. Bell had not been so forthright to announce that he purchased the crutches, but he had not corrected Elizabeth when she expressed her gratitude, either.

I rose to leave. "Thank you, doctor."

"Will I see you at the demonstration this evening?"

"You certainly shall."

I returned immediately to the museum and went straight to Dorfoy's office. I did not wait for him to answer my knock, but opened the door and walked in.

"Mr. Watson. You are late."

"Is Dr. Bell in the building?"

"I don't expect him until directly before his demonstration. I do need you to take care of a few things."

"I must find Bell."

"He is away on business. He did not say where. Why the urgency?"

Obviously Dorfoy was unaware of Elizabeth's news. I collected myself. "I did not mean to sound urgent. I suppose it was my being late that made it appear so."

"You'll need to wait to speak with him until before he goes on stage. But catch him then, because he leaves early on Tuesday."

Oh, how I knew that already.

I spent the day avoiding Elizabeth. I had nothing to say to her, at least until I had evidence that supported my inclinations about Bell's character. If I found nothing, I knew I could do little to stop her, and I did not understand her desperation. She and Enos would be in the grand hall until early evening, so I stayed in the theater, working with Thomas and Ginny to ready the space. Dorfoy expected an enormous crowd this evening, since word of mouth spread about Bell's prior performance. Everyone wanted to be examined by the famous doctor of phrenology, or at least to see others' characters revealed in public. The more outrageous the better, and apparently Bell's distasteful judgment of my character had piqued their interest. People loved to see others fall.

"Mr. Watson," called Thomas, "reckon you could help me move these chairs?"

I walked to the middle of the theater. Bell had asked that two aisles be created, to allow him more access to the audience. We moved the heavy wooden chairs to open new aisles that ended near the back of the room, where people sat on long benches rather than chairs. As we rearranged, Ginny swept around us with a broom.

"I can't use a mop this time of year," she muttered, "water would freeze." Only one stove heated the large room, but it would not be lit until performance time. "Thomas, you remember the time I washed up the vestibule floor and Mr. Dorfoy near threw out his back?"

Thomas laughed under his breath.

"It was not funny, Thomas."

I imagined the dignified Dorfoy sprawled on the floor, his top hat askew.

Just then, Dorfoy entered the theater. "Fabulous! Fabulous," he said, removing a pair of gloves as he walked up one of the side aisles. "Could we fit some more chairs along the walls?"

Thomas grumbled that this was possible and exited through the door next to the stage.

"Ginny, could you work on cleaning the entry hall? It's a trifle dusty."

"Certainly, Mr. Dorfoy." She, too, left the theater.

"So, Mr. Watson," Dorfoy turned to me. "Mrs. Stutsman came by my office a short while ago."

"She did?"

"She says she is leaving with Mr. Bell tomorrow. He

has given her a marriage proposal." He looked at me expectantly.

Marriage! It had gone as far as I imagined. But why had she not told me?

"I see. And what do you think of this, Mr. Dorfoy?

"I hardly have much to say about it. It has been a small space of time since they met, but stranger things have happened in love. Besides, the public will grow tired of Enos and crave something new. Sensation is always short lived, my boy."

I said nothing in return.

"What do you think, Mr. Watson?"

"I wish them all the happiness in the world."

"I don't believe you."

My reserve crumbled. "I think he's a conniving, unscrupulous, manipulative…"

"Aha! I knew it!" Dorfoy began laughing.

"Sir?"

"I knew it. You're in love with her. Despite the little you know of her."

"Sir, I've hardly had time to…"

"As I said, stranger things have happened in love."

"But she loves Bell."

"Are you sure of it?"

"I am too young. I have no money. You have not paid me a penny since I've come here."

"Let us not change the subject, now," he said, holding his hand up in protest. "I've seen how she looks at you. Dr. Bell's charms can mystify a woman. Perhaps you need to break the spell."

"They leave in the morning."

"The morning is still hours away. Bell returned a short while ago and is in the dining room having a drink."

I found Bell seated at the table with a jug of whiskey and a glass before him. "Mr. Watson! Please, have a seat."

"I understand congratulations are in order," I said.

"Would you care for a drink?"

"No," I replied. "Did you not hear? I just offered my congratulations."

"And they are heartily accepted." He took a drink.

"Do you love her?" I asked.

"Love. Such a complicated brew of emotions."

"Bell!" I pounded my fist on the table. "Do you love her?"

He looked completely unshaken. "She needs me."

"And you need her."

"Very perceptive. She will make a wonderful, dutiful wife, no doubt."

I could only stare at him.

"Do not fear, Watson. I shall take care of her."

"And what of her son?"

"Enos shall get the education he deserves. That is, of course, between traveling. My occupation takes me all over the country. You can't expect my wife and her child to exist without me that often. Besides, they are already accustomed to the kind of life I lead."

"And what kind of life is that?" I asked.

He lifted his glass to his lips and set it down again. "Why, the showman's life."

"That is exactly the kind of life Elizabeth is trying to escape."

"Is it? Then what is she doing here? If she thinks Enos draws crowds here, at Dorfoy's pathetic museum, she will be more than pleased to see the audiences that will pay to see him in Boston and Philadelphia, and even New York."

I stood up and nearly knocked over my chair. "You cannot be serious."

"Calm down, Watson! I assure you, my new show will be entirely scientific. I have been exploring the applications of phrenology to the fitness of the entire body. The body houses the soul, after all."

I could scarcely believe what I was hearing. Elizabeth was convinced that she would be given a home for her and her son and that they would soon leave behind this life. Dr. Bell's intentions were completely the opposite. He had sensed Elizabeth's desperation and pounced. My head felt as if it would explode. My breath sped up, and it took all my resolve to not spring across the table and smash this man to the floor. Instead, I clenched my fists at my side and resolved to hide my anger. I would find a way to diffuse his plans tonight. I sat back down.

"So, it seems you have it all sorted out," I said.

"Why yes, of course. The show is my livelihood. Without it, I cannot support a wife and son."

"But of course. A toast, then." I squeezed out a smile.

Bell reached for another glass and poured me a small amount of whiskey.

"A toast." He raised his glass, and we both drank.

# Chapter 30
## The Final Demonstration

*Arthur Watson*

By the time I reached the theater, there was standing room only. People filled every seat in the house and had already begun to line up along the walls around the room. A din of excitement hung in the air—people laughed and talked, their voices echoing in the high-ceilinged space. I looked to the front row for Elizabeth and Enos and was surprised not to see them there. Surely Bell would have reserved seats for them. I searched the crowd from my vantage point at the back of the theater. Finally, my eyes alighted on a small woman in blue waving to get my attention. It was Elizabeth, seated along the opposite aisle, about mid way back from the stage. I made my way over to speak with her.

"Good evening, Mrs. Stutsman. Greetings, Enos. And, why, good evening to you as well, Ginny. How kind of Mr. Dorfoy to give you this evening off."

The boy's face lit up. "Dr. Bell is going to call mama to the stage!"

Shocked, I looked at Elizabeth.

"Only if I raise my hand, Enos." She shook her head. "I'm not sure I'll feel up to it."

"Why would he ask you to do such a thing?" I asked.

"He gets very few women volunteers. He asked politely, and I told him I would consider it."

"I would do it," said Enos, disappointment in his voice.

"As would I, lad," said Ginny.

"Enos," Elizabeth said, "I told you that Dr. Bell and I discussed this and agreed it would not be proper for a child." Enos crossed his arms and slouched in his chair.

"I'm so sorry, Mr. Watson," she continued, "that we did not keep a seat for you. After the last demonstration, I did not expect to see you here." Of course, she would wonder why in Heaven's name I would subject myself to another so-called analysis by Bell. That was the least of my concerns now.

"I'm perfectly fine standing." I traced the mounting line of people, mostly men, along the walls. "I'd better go find a place if I'm to see the show at all." I began to walk away, but thinking better of it, I turned back and said, "Mrs. Stutsman?"

"Yes?"

"Might I have a word with you after the demonstration?"

"Of course, Mr. Watson," she said with a glimmer in her eye, or perhaps I imagined that.

"Enjoy the show, Mr. Watson," called Ginny as I set off to find a good spot from which to watch.

I pushed my way through throngs of people standing in the aisles along the walls until I found a vacant space entirely on the opposite side of the theater from

Elizabeth. From there I could see the stage quite well, on which stood a single wooden chair before a red curtain. I also had a clear view of the blue sheen of the shoulders of Elizabeth's dress and her lovely profile. Enos turned to give me a little wave and a smile, and I nodded back to him. No sooner had I taken my place than Mr. Dorfoy came through the red curtain. The crowd quickly fell silent.

"Good evening, my friends, and welcome. How wonderful to see some familiar faces and many new ones. Ladies, gentlemen, on this illustrious occasion I am proud to once again present the talented Dr. Damien Bell from Boston, Mass."

A sullen man standing next to me muttered, "I can't believe I paid money for this nonsense." His eyes were dark and deep set as he glared at Dorfoy.

Dorfoy continued. "After Dr. Bell's demonstration, which is guaranteed to astound, I invite you to be further amazed by the Infernal Regions, which will remain open late this evening to accommodate tonight's landmark crowd."

The audience applauded and cheered, save for the man next to me, who pulled a flask out of his jacket, took a drink, and wiped his face with a dirty sleeve. I studied his countenance for a moment. He appeared several years older than I and would have been handsome if not for his scowl, which seemed permanently writ on his face. I thought comically for a moment how fascinating it would be to see Bell analyze him. The applause subsided as Dorfoy left the stage. After an appropriately dramatic pause, the red curtain opened, revealing the two large drawings of a human head. Bell appeared from behind the banners, smug as ever.

"Greetings fair citizens of Cincinnati, and salutations to those who have traveled from afar." I could not fathom anyone coming from so far away to see Bell's little routine. He continued to repeat the same dialogue he had during his previous demonstration, explaining with aplomb the value of phrenology, the importance of character, and the ability for men to improve their flaws once they were made aware of them. His voice faded into the background as my attention turned to Elizabeth. I noticed the stick-straight way she proudly sat in her chair, the way her nose pointed up ever so slightly up at the tip, the shine of her straw-colored hair pulled back by the silk flower behind her delicate ear. Just then, she turned my way. At first, she smiled, but suddenly her mouth opened in shock. She lifted her hand to her lips in surprise. What was it? I had done nothing. Her gaze was locked in my direction. She leaned over to whisper something in Ginny's ear. Then, as if called by a voice only she could hear, she rose quickly from her chair.

Bell had just swept his arms wide, as if to embrace the audience. "Tonight, I will select directly from you, my genial audience. And—oh—already? A volunteer. A lovely lady! How wonderful! I so rarely get the privilege of analyzing a lady." He gestured toward Elizabeth. But instead of walking toward the stage, she turned quickly and nearly ran from the theater. Enos began to ready his crutches, but I saw Ginny restrain and reassure him.

Before the doors closed behind Elizabeth, the surly man next to me grunted, looked around quickly, and made a quiet exit into the corridor through the doors immediately behind us. By now I was so confused I hardly knew what was happening.

Elizabeth's leaving ruffled Bell. He stood in a rare moment of confusion, his face red and pinched. "Perhaps I was mistaken. It seems our lady had an emergency." Chuckles rose from the crowd, but he immediately regained his composure. "Now, for some genuine volunteers?" Hands shot up around the theater. I heard Bell select a young man from the second row as I followed Elizabeth out through the theater's side doors.

"Elizabeth?" I called. I looked around but saw no one. I walked quietly toward the entrance hall. Before rounding the corner, I heard the voices of a man and a woman. I paused to listen.

"You must have known I would come for you," said a gruff voice I recognized as belonging to the man who had stood next to me in the audience.

"Hans, you must leave." It was Elizabeth, her voice surprisingly calm. I searched my memory for that name— Hans.

"You're coming with me," he demanded.

"I shall not," she replied stiffly.

"I've fed you and that boy for almost a year. You will come!"

"We are never coming back."

I was about to intercede, but as my shoulder turned the corner, something the man said made me stop.

"Listen to me! He may be monstrous and deformed, but he is my own flesh and blood. I will have my son under my own roof and you there to care for him."

Suddenly, my mind returned to the day in the cosmorama when Elizabeth confided in me. Hans was her brother. I was certain this to be correct. But Enos is his son? How? My stomach dropped, and I felt as if I would vomit. Confusion made my head reel. Perhaps the old women in the grand hall were correct, and Enos suffered from the sins of his parents.

Elizabeth's voice started to quiver. "He is not a monster. Your home is no place for us."

"Whore!" he yelled. "What other ways are you earning a living here? Whoring around with the other freaks at the museum and that queer Frenchman who runs the place? You disgust me. Even Jacob, that useless husband of yours, would have spit on you had he not been so weak as to die."

"You filthy, stinking man!" she cried. "How can I even call you a man. You are a demon with whiskey in his veins. I cook and clean for you, and for what? Enos has nothing back there. The first time you struck me, we were already gone."

I began to approach them, hoping the dispute would not escalate, but they were several lengths before me, and the tall display cases obscured my presence.

"I should have taken the boy the other night. If I had not left Enos on the street, you'd have come groveling back to me," he sneered.

I squinted at his face, and suddenly the air went from

my lungs. I had seen the man at the river after all, in the split second his boot hit my chest. It had been Hans. He must have heard Bell calling Enos's name and panicked, leaving Enos in the alley.

"Go back to the theater and get the boy," he said, grabbing Elizabeth by the wrist.

"I will do no such thing!" She twisted her thin arm from his grasp and, freeing herself, began running toward the stairs at the back of the entrance hall, her blue dress billowing behind her.

# Chapter 31
## The Infernal Regions

*Elizabeth Stutsman*

I ran with all my might but could hear Hans' heavy footsteps approaching quickly. There was nowhere to go and no one to help me. All were inside the theater, and I felt utterly alone. I saw the stairs ahead of me and grabbed my skirt, lifting it to my knees. My legs steadily carried me up, and while each step seemed an eternity, I hardly knew I was running. I heard Hans stumble on the stairs and thought I could hear him breathing. I began to think about where I would go once in the grand hall. Was there a room with a door I could block shut? Perhaps the cosmorama? The hall of gems? Suddenly, I heard a shuffle and thud. Hans had tripped, his legs unsteady from too much drink.

"Hell!" he shouted.

He got up instantly, but I had gained some time, a few seconds at least. When I reached the top, I saw the stage on the left, where Enos and I had whiled away the past several days. The hall was lit with a few lamps, but the rooms on either side were dark. I could slip into one of them, but it was too late. Hans had emerged from the staircase. He laughed when he saw me.

"You can't hide," he said, glowering like an angry bull.

We both stood, staring each other down across the grand hall. Hans tried to catch his breath. He bent low and hung his arms out to either side with palms forward as if he were trying to catch a runaway child or a small animal. I glanced over my shoulder and saw the double doors in the far corner. Dorfoy had said the Infernal Regions would be open late this evening. Thomas or Mr. Powers could be there readying the display. I ran to the doors, hoping they would be unlocked. I grabbed the handle, and to my relief, it turned and clicked.

"Thomas?" I shouted anxiously. There was no answer. Hans' footsteps quickened behind me, so I ducked inside the door and pulled it shut. I jiggled the handle, hoping to be able to lock it, to no avail. I had expected total darkness, but a bit of dim light shone from the top of the narrow, steep stairs that ascended to the terrible attic. Ginny, in her desire to see Dr. Bell's demonstration, must have lit the lamps before his performance.

"Thomas?" I called again. Nothing. He was not here.

If I could get to the top of the stairs before Hans opened the door, I might have a chance to hide within the huge display. There were certainly plenty of dark corners. I took a deep breath and bounded up the steps. When I reached the top, I gave my eyes a moment to adjust. The Regions looked nothing like it had my first time through. The lifeless automatons at the entrance, now more pathetic than terrifying, stood dully in the dim lamplight. I began to inch forward, taking care not to lose my footing. My arm bumped into something cold and thin. I jumped back—it was the wire barrier, thankfully as of yet not electrified. I grasped the wire and ran my hand along it to guide myself in the near darkness, listening for any sounds from the stairs. My hand brushed something cool and rough—a rock outcropping into which the wire ran. I felt my way around it and found a cave-like hole low to the ground. I crouched and worked myself into the opening. My breath seemed so loud, and my heart pounded in my ears. I closed my eyes and worked hard to slow my breathing.

I then heard footsteps. My hiding place was so dark I could not tell whether or not I had opened my eyes, but in a moment I sensed the faint, red glow from the lamps along the walkway. How I prayed the footsteps belonged to Thomas. He would tell me he chased away Hans, and that Enos was safe with Ginny or Mr. Dorfoy. I sat as still as the boulders around me.

"Elizabeth," Hans hissed. "I know you think you can outsmart me, but you are wrong. I will find you, and when I do..." His footsteps came closer. He now stood right in front of me, and I could see the mud-encrusted heels of his boots.

Suddenly, another voice rang out like a point of light in the darkness. "Leave her alone!" It was Arthur. He was attempting to sound fierce, but his voice wavered. Hans turned sharply, and what little I could see of him disappeared again into the shadows. I stayed huddled in my corner, trying to visualize what was happening.

"This business is not yours, boy," snapped Hans.

"Elizabeth is my business," Arthur replied.

"Hah!" Hans mocked, "Elizabeth has a lover."

"She is my friend," said Arthur. "And you will leave her alone."

Hans let out almost a growl. Scuffling sounds followed. I heard sickening thuds that must have been fists falling on flesh and bodies slamming against walls. I could sit quietly no longer.

"Stop!" I cried, pulling myself up.

They completely ignored me. The light was just potent enough to catch the outlines of their thrashing bodies. I could barely tell them apart. Elbows pulled back and thrust forward as punches landed on jaws. They grunted and groaned like animals as they grabbed at each other's clothing. Then their motions slowed. I saw Hans, who was the larger of the two, pushing Arthur away. As they turned, I could finally see that Hans' hands were around Arthur's throat, slowly crushing the air from it.

"Stop it! Please!" I began to feel along the wall for something, anything, with which to hit Hans. My hand came to something among the fabricated rocks. It was a long, cast iron poker, a prop to stoke the fires of this imaginary Inferno. I grasped it tightly in both hands and raised it over my head. But it was heavy, and as I brought it down, Hans shifted to the right. Instead of making contact with his skull, it fell weakly on his shoulder. My action did not render him unconscious, but it did make him release Arthur, who fell to the ground wheezing and clutching at his neck.

"You foul woman!" Hans turned on me and instantly wrenched the poker from my hands. I backed slowly away at first, then turned and began running deeper into the Regions, hoping not to fall into one of the ghoulish dioramas, which were lit more brightly than the entrance. It was in front of the Devil himself where Hans caught me. Lucifer loomed atop his mountain of boulders and grinned morbidly down at us when Hans grabbed the collar of my dress and jolted me backwards. He wrapped his arm around my neck and held me close to his body, nearly lifting my feet from the ground. He held the poker in his other hand and pointed it between my breasts.

"Arthur!" I yelled. "Stay where you are."

"Quiet," Hans said through clenched teeth into my ear. His breath smelled of whiskey, tobacco, and rotted meat. He tightened his grip on my neck.

Demons leered all around us. Tortured souls, begging for redemption, now seemed to plead for mercy on my very own soul.

"We have quite an audience, my dear," snorted Hans.

"It's exactly where you belong," I replied. He responded by lifting the handle of the poker, poising it to spear through me.

"You were like my brother once," I continued, a tear spilling over my cheek, "and then I gave myself to you. Can you not find it deep within your heart to have pity?"

"You betrayed me long ago, and now again. How can you expect me to trust you?"

"Elizabeth!" Arthur emerged into the reddish glow.

"Stay back," warned Hans, renewing his force on the poker.

Arthur put his hands up, palms forward. "Calm down. I only want you to let her go."

"I said stay back!"

I felt faint but kept my head. I needed to see that Arthur was safe. Hans dragged me backwards, closer to the evil display. Arthur moved sideways, nearing the diorama of wax devils across from us.

Suddenly, another voice bellowed from near the entrance. "What in blazes is goin' on up here? You better stop. I got a pistol."

"Thomas!" I cried.

"Shut up!" Hans tightened his arm around my neck, then lifted the poker high and brought it down on my head.

# Chapter 32
## A Horrific Sight

*Arthur Watson*

I saw Elizabeth crumple to the floor.

"No!" I screamed and lunged for Hans. With all my weight, I shoved him hard into the wall, and he hit his head with a crack. He was stunned, but it was not enough to stop him. He brought up his hand and pushed it into my face, forcing my nose upward until I had to give. Before I could think, he spun around, and in one fell swoop grabbed my arm, twisted it behind my back, and pressed my cheek against the wall's rough, stone-like surface.

"I could break it, you know."

He pulled up hard, and my arm felt as if it would come apart. Just as a hot flash of pain leaped through my shoulder, a gunshot rang out. Startled, Hans loosened his grip and freed my arm.

"Stop it right there," said Thomas, wielding his pistol in Hans' direction.

Hans didn't move. I caught my breath and began to move slowly away.

"You all right Mr. Watson?" asked Thomas, who had the gun trained on Hans.

"Sure."

"Good. Now, check on Mrs. Stutsman."

I rushed over to her collapsed body. To my relief, her chest fell and rose. "She's unconscious," I answered. Blood matted her hair where the iron had struck her scalp. I removed my jacket, rolled it up, and placed it under her head. As I arranged her limbs so she could rest more comfortably, a loud clicking sound came out of the darkness.

The sound distracted Thomas for a second, and Hans took the opportunity to make a move. In a flash he reached down and picked up the poker. Seeming as if his feet weren't even on the ground, he flew forward with the poker poised toward Thomas. A gunshot cut through the air. The bullet pierced Hans' left knee, sending his body falling into the diorama. The iron poker still in his hand landed on the wire barrier, and his body began convulsing and writhing.

"We have to pull him off!" I yelled.

"Don't touch him!" screamed Thomas, "or you'll sure as heck be roasted, too."

It was a horrific sight. I was grateful Elizabeth was unconscious, as the scene would certainly have recurred in her nightmares for the rest of her life. Hans' face went tight, his eyes rolled up so that only the whites were visible, and his body stiffened. The smell was something so putrid, so vile, I cannot even describe it.

While we stood helpless around Hans' flailing body, a figure rushed in from the direction opposite the entrance. It was Mr. Powers. He held a long, wooden pole in his strong sculptor's arms. He placed the pole underneath the iron poker and lifted it off the wire. Hans's body went limp, slumping to the ground face first. Mr. Powers knelt and rolled him over, placing his hand in front of Hans' nose and mouth.

"I was too late," he said. "He's no longer breathing."

Thomas and I now sat on the ground as well, staring at Hans.

"I was in the back, turning on the electrified fence to get ready to open," continued Mr. Powers. "It's my fault. I've been experimenting with the currents."

"He would have killed them both," said Thomas. "And me, too, if he would've had a chance. I got no doubt about that. You saved them, Mr. Powers."

Thomas leaned down and closed Hans' eyes with his fingers. "Who was he?" he asked.

"I am not exactly certain," I replied, moving back over to Elizabeth. I crouched next to her. "Thomas, she will need the doctor."

I lifted her small hand and held it. "Mrs. Stutsman? Can you hear me?"

She swallowed. "Elizabeth?" I touched her cheek.

Her head moved just a little, and her eyes began to flutter lightly behind her eyelids.

"Arthur? Where's Enos?" Her eyes flung open.

"Stay still, Elizabeth. Enos is safe, but you're hurt quite badly. Thomas has gone to the theater to fetch Dr. Drake." She reached up and felt her head, and let out a small moan.

"Just lay back and rest. I will stay with you until the

doctor arrives."

She leaned her head back down on my jacket. "Where is Hans?" she asked.

"Stay calm, Elizabeth. Hans is... he is dead."

She inhaled deeply and looked off into the distance.

"Was he, indeed, your brother?" I was compelled to ask.

"I did call him brother once," she said, and closed her eyes. My head filled with confusion, I restrained myself from asking any further questions. He said he was Enos's father. But Elizabeth's brother? The reality of this possibility set in, and I struggled to grasp it. It could not be possible. Not Elizabeth. It simply could not be true. And yet, Enos's condition seemed to suggest that it could be. Horrible things happened to punish people who committed such acts. The children of such unions were deformed and defiled. But Enos was a smart, kind boy. I could not make sense of this. My mind reeled. Elizabeth needed to recover, so I would press her on it later, and not so publicly.

"I will find Mr. Dorfoy and tell him the Regions must not be opened this evening," said Mr. Powers. "He would not want this scene to sully the reputation of the museum."

I waited silently with Elizabeth. After what seemed like an eternity, I could hear people running up the stairs.

"What has happened?" demanded Dorfoy.

"I will explain everything," I said. "First, Mrs. Stutsman needs the doctor's attention."

Dr. Drake knelt down next to Elizabeth. "Can you

hear me, my dear?" he asked. Elizabeth opened her eyes. "Good. Very good," he said. "Can you move your fingers?" She carefully lifted her hand and rested it on her stomach. "Wonderful. Now, can you move your legs?" She shifted them around beneath her dress. "Now, we are going to help you sit up. Mr. Watson, will you please brace her under her arm?" The two of us helped her to a vertical position.

"I feel dizzy," she said, "and nauseous."

"That is to be expected after trauma to your head," said Dr. Drake.

She looked down at her blood soaked sleeve and the small red puddle on the floor then flung her eyes toward the doctor, terrified.

"Calm down, Mrs. Stutsman. It appears much worse that it is. The scalp bleeds profusely when it is damaged." He felt her skull gently, and Elizabeth whimpered. "I feel no significant damage. It is only a surface wound. You're going to be just fine." He pressed a cloth on her head. "Mr. Watson, hold this here with some pressure to quell the bleeding. She may need some sutures."

"Where is Hans?" she asked.

Not sure she could handle seeing him, I replied, "Really, Mrs. Stutsman, perhaps you should rest. You're not in any condition to move right now."

"I must see him!" she said, her strength more apparent than I believed possible.

"I think we can help her to her feet," said the doctor. "Careful, careful," he said, as we assisted her.

"He is over there," I said, gesturing toward the

diorama. I took her arm and we walked slowly over to the body.

"Oh!" she exclaimed, raising her hand to cover her nose and mouth. I pulled out my handkerchief and offered it to her. "What happened?" she asked.

"He went after Thomas with the poker, and Thomas shot him in the leg. Hans fell into the wire barrier, which had been electrified for the evening's visitors. Elizabeth, I'm sorry to say he was electrocuted."

She said nothing, but just looked down at him with dark and vacant eyes. Then, her gaze alighted on a gleaming bit of white poking out of Hans' breast pocket. She leaned down and plucked out a small card. She turned it over and saw that it was Dorfoy's calling card.

"I must have dropped it. I led him straight to us." She turned away and buried her head in my chest. I patted her back to console her.

"Mrs. Stutsman," said Thomas, "I beg pardon, but he wouldn't have stopped. He'd have killed us all. I could see it in his eyes."

"I know, Thomas," she replied. "I know. There was a good man inside, long buried beneath the man he became." She turned back into me.

More steps came bounding up the stairs. From the shadows emerged Bell.

"Elizabeth!" he shouted. "Where are you?"

When he arrived at the scene, his face went pale. He first looked to the dead man on the floor, then to Elizabeth cradled in my arms, then back to the corpse.

"What in the hell has happened here?"

Elizabeth pulled away from me.

"Who is this man?" Bell demanded, not even for an instant attempting to comfort Elizabeth, who stood there staring at him.

"He was my brother," she said calmly, "with whom Enos and I stayed after my husband passed."

Bell looked utterly confused. "Have you nothing to say, Watson?"

"What Elizabeth says is true."

"Then why is he lying dead on the floor?"

"He fell into the electric barrier," I said.

Elizabeth walked toward Bell. "Hans had a problem with whiskey," she said. "He became belligerent and violent, so Enos and I came here. It is over now," she said, and stroked Bell's cheek. He reached up and stopped her hand.

"I see," he said. "What kind of family do you come from?" he asked. Elizabeth's jaw dropped. "I know nothing of you. It appears you may have killed a man or at least played accomplice. I cannot have a scandal follow me. I have my career to consider."

"Hans was all the family I had left," said Elizabeth, whose voice now shook pathetically. She took Bell's hand once again.

"Elizabeth, look at your head," said Bell, whose tone now changed to one of compassion. "You are in no condition to travel so soon. I will not allow you to accompany me tomorrow. I must take some time to think about this, as well."

My feelings for Elizabeth were now so convoluted. A

flurry of emotions ripped through me, but I could not stand by to listen to Bell's reprimands. She had even fewer options now. Although I knew he had ulterior motives, I also now knew Elizabeth's secret and I was not sure I could forgive it.

"Bell—you made her a promise," I said. "You cannot leave her behind. And what about Enos?"

"It was no promise," he retorted. "It was simply an offer, which I now withdraw." With that, he dropped Elizabeth's hand and made his way back into the darkness and down the stairs. Elizabeth stood there, stunned.

"Mrs. Stutsman," said Dorfoy, "you and your son may stay with me for as long as you like." His face appeared sympathetic now.

"Thank you," she returned. "Mr. Watson, would you kindly help me downstairs to see my boy?" She extended her arm to me, and I took her elbow.

"Dr. Drake," said Dorfoy, gesturing toward Hans' disheveled body. "I assume you can do something about this?" The doctor nodded without a sound.

# Chapter 33
## The Most Talented Seamstress

*Elizabeth Stutsman*

Spring must be the loveliest time of year in Cincinnati. After the long, gray winter, the hills around the city sparkled with tiny leaves sprouting like emeralds in the balmy air. The scent of rain hung in the breeze, and showers came to wash away the dust in the city streets. The steamboats brought more visitors who flitted in and out of shops and taverns. The warmer weather also increased the stench from the slaughterhouses, but fortune located my shop on the western edge of town, where only just the right wind direction carries the odor.

It was on such a warm, breezy, rainy day that I sat in my shop working on a dress—an elaborate construction out of yellow silks from England for a very refined acquaintance of Dr. Drake. The doctor has been very kind, sending many customers my way. Mr. Dorfoy, although disappointed when Enos and I took our leave of the museum, rejoiced that Cincinnati had not lost us to Boston and already calls me the most talented seamstress in the city. His opinion and influence have not hurt business, either.

I was sitting with my back to the entrance, stitching on a sleeve, when the door flew open. I turned to see a young man with his hat pulled low, his collar up, carrying a pile of clothing.

"So good to be finally out of the rain!" he exclaimed in a familiar voice. When he lifted his head from its bent position to keep the rain off his face, I saw it was Arthur. My heart stopped. I had not seen him for two months, since he had left the museum in haste after the horrific occurrence in the Infernal Regions. I stood up and laid the dress gently down on my worktable. Arthur froze, looking at me as if he had seen a ghost.

"Greetings, Mr. Watson," I said, keeping my composure as best I could.

"Good day, Mrs. Stutsman. I didn't know this was your shop."

"Why, yes. I have been here since March."

"One of my colleagues at the bank suggested I bring my jackets and shirts here. They are in dire need of mending."

I was stunned at how quickly our surprise meeting had become strictly business.

"Bring them here." I motioned with my hand, and Arthur walked over. "They're awfully damp," I said, unfolding the items and draping them over the back of a chair.

"The rain," said Arthur, laughing slightly. His face was as gentle and handsome as ever. His acts of kindness came flooding back to me, and I chastised myself for being so severe to him.

"This won't take more than two or three days," I replied, writing up a ticket for him.

"You look well," he said.

"I am getting on just fine."

"How is Enos?"

"He is growing quickly. He is in school." I said this proudly because not only was he in school but he was at the head of his class.

"How wonderful! He will do very well."

We were both silent for a moment. Arthur looked down at his shoes and finally said, "I must be going back to work. It is a busy time."

"Are you working at the Branch Bank?"

"No—Franklin. The gentlemen who have incorporated the Lafayette Bank have spoken to me as well, enlisting me to help them when they open in autumn, but I like Franklin and intend to stay there, at least for a while."

"I am glad you are making a way for yourself. I know it is all you ever wanted."

Arthur paused a moment. "It is almost all I ever wanted." His eyes caught mine, and he smiled slightly.

"I will have these ready for you by Thursday. You may pick them up, or if you prefer, I could bring them by the bank after I meet Enos at school."

"If the weather is pleasant, perhaps you could come by. I would love to see Enos."

"Very well then. I will see you Thursday afternoon."

He tipped his hat, bid me good day, and ducked out of the shop. I sat back down and picked up the dress but just held it in my lap. Arthur's reappearance shook me. After he left the museum so suddenly, with only so much as a nod of his head and a quick embrace for Enos, I worked hard to keep him out of my mind. I couldn't blame him. I had agreed to marry Dr. Bell, and I am certain the emergence of Hans and the violence of that evening had placed me in a different light. However, there must be something else. How could his ardor have cooled so rapidly?

# Chapter 34
## Elizabeth's Secret

*Arthur Watson*

I t had been a little more than two months since I left Dorfoy and the museum. There was no future for me in that world of exploitation, so I gave Dorfoy my notice the day after Elizabeth's confrontation with Hans, on the same day Bell left Elizabeth to find her own direction. While I think Dorfoy is a naturalist at heart, his appetite for the sensational did not suit me in the least.

I have told no one what I overheard the night of Hans' death. Such knowledge would destroy Elizabeth, and even worse, Enos. The boy is an innocent and has much potential to make something of himself. I could not be the harbinger of ill to them. Having said that, I could also no longer pursue Elizabeth. Dorfoy was correct when he told me I knew nothing of her character. I could still not help but wonder about the circumstances and I resolved to ask her when I was able.

That moment came on a warm spring afternoon. I had not predicted my visit to a seamstress would renew my society with Elizabeth, yet there she was, looking lovely as ever, her lap piled with a shimmering yellow dress, more like the petals of a sunflower than the wheaten color of her hair. We exchanged pleasantries, but I would see her again when she delivered my mended clothes. I was writing the day's last entries into my account book when I looked up and saw her step into the bank. In her arms she carried a bundle wrapped in paper and tied with string, and next to her walked Enos, looking taller already and very manly in a little suit, his body held high and straight with his crutches.

"Good day!" I called. "I'll be with you in a moment." I quickly finished up my record keeping and reached for my hat.

"Mr. Watson!" called Enos, waving frantically. I walked over and patted him on the head.

"Enos—you have grown so much in the past months. Your mother tells me you are attending school." I took the package from Elizabeth, and the three of us began walking to the door.

"Yes. It is great fun. I walk there myself, and I have friends, and..."

"And he is doing very well in his studies," Elizabeth interrupted.

"Oh, yes, that, too," said Enos sheepishly as we emerged onto the street.

"Enos's teacher tells me he could have a future in education or even in law."

"I've never doubted you would do great things, Enos." He smiled widely, and Elizabeth beamed at him.

"Mama—can I run ahead to the general store to buy some penny candy?"

"Certainly, Enos," she said, handing him a few coins. He flew off before I could even offer him some coins of my own.

Elizabeth and I walked on a few paces. I held my elbow out for her, and she took it with her thin hand. She wore a comely dress, not fancy, but well-made and fashionable, most likely one of her own design.

"How long have you worked at the seamstress shop?" I asked.

"Work there, Mr. Watson? I own it." She could see the surprise in my face. "I know, it seems impossible. I was willing to run off to Boston because we had not a penny to our name. I found an investor."

"An investor? Not Mr. Dorfoy?"

"Heavens, no. He still struggles to keep the museum open. I'm speaking of Mr. Longworth."

"Of course! Mr. Longworth. I saw he was a kind man the minute I laid eyes on him."

"Even more, he took quite an interest in Enos. He wrote the letter of introduction that gained us admittance to the school. He told us that when he saw such young intellect, he could not bear to see it go to waste."

"How wonderful."

"It was Mr. Longworth who purchased the crutches after all."

I thought of Bell's underhandedness. "Have you heard from Dr. Bell?"

She laughed. "I do not expect to. If I should, I'll send him running back to Boston."

"It seemed you were quite serious."

"I was desperate."

We walked on a little further. The question gnawed at the inside of my skull until finally I approached it.

"Mrs. Stutsman, I regret I never fully expressed my sympathies to you about your brother's death. I know the situation was complicated, and I failed to know exactly what to say."

"I understand. It is over now, and in the past. I have let that terrible evening go, and you should as well."

I swallowed hard. "Pardon my forthrightness, but I still do not grasp your relationship to your brother."

We stopped, and she looked at me. "What do you mean? Our relationship?"

I took her hand and pulled her to a small alcove between two buildings.

"What is it, Mr. Watson?"

"Mrs. Stutsman, I must confess that I overheard you speaking to Hans that night, when the two of you were in the corridor outside the theater." Her face went white, and I shifted uncomfortably. "I distinctly heard Hans say that he was Enos's father, and you did not object. I can hardly believe he could be both your brother and the boy's father."

"Stop," she said. "I do not wish to speak of this further." She turned to walk back into the street, but I grabbed her arm. Realizing I had been too harsh, I just as quickly dropped it.

"Elizabeth—please. I only want to understand."

She gazed into my eyes, and finally said, "All right."

I listened as she told me of her childhood once again, of her brother Hans who was dearest to her of all people and his imminent downfall. I had heard most of the story before, but that day in the museum, which now seemed an eternity ago, she had omitted some critical details.

"My father had a stable hand whose wife had died in childbirth, leaving the poor man to raise his infant son alone," Elizabeth related, in our private little alcove sheltered from the street. "When his son was still less than a year old, the stable hand died of cholera. My father convinced my mother to raise the boy as their own."

"Hans," I said.

"You already know how close Hans and I were until whiskey consumed him."

"Yes." I listened intently.

"I loved him as my brother, even though our entire family knew he was not of our flesh and blood. As Hans and I grew older, our feelings became confused. My parents would not have understood if we had become romantically attached. Hans and I felt it best if he found work and started a life of his own, and if I gave in to the attentions of a suitor who had been pursuing me for some time."

"And then Hans returned a drunkard."

"At first, yes. But, months later, he claimed he had reformed. He returned again for a few weeks, and we spent every possible minute together. We were both just eighteen, and one night, we lost ourselves. He went back to work at the mill, and weeks later, I suspected I was with child."

"And you told Hans?"

"He visited us shortly thereafter, and, yes, I told him. He stormed out. That evening, he joined his old friends at a tavern. One night of drinking was all it took to send him headlong into ruin."

"Oh, Elizabeth."

"Now you see why I did not tell you. Enos was conceived out of wedlock. I was a ruined woman."

"But you did marry."

"Yes. I married the man who had been my suitor—Jacob Stutsman, a family friend much older than I. He was kind and, because of his age, eager to marry. I allowed him, and everyone else, to believe that Enos was his child."

"And he loved Enos, from what you have told me."

"Oh, yes. He loved Enos more than anything, even more than he loved me. And I grew to love Jacob. We moved to Philadelphia when Enos was still an infant, and our family shared a happy life there. By the time Jacob died, my parents were already gone, and I had nowhere else to turn. I found Hans in Indiana, and he invited us to stay."

She was shaking by now. I grabbed her shoulders and pulled her into my embrace. She sobbed into my chest.

"Say no more, Elizabeth," I said, stroking her hair. "I know the rest."

We stood there for a few moments, until she pulled away from me, smoothed her hair, and pinched her cheeks to bring back some color. "We should catch up with Enos now."

We walked back out onto the street, where people bustled to and fro as if we had never left. The sun shone low in the sky as horses clopped by, and shopkeepers began turning their signs around to read "closed." Elizabeth held my arm and leaned against me. Up ahead, I could see Enos ambling toward us on two crutches, several peppermint sticks jutting out of his pocket.

As he approached, he propped one crutch against his body, grabbed the candy, and lifted it high into the air. "Look, Mama and Mr. Watson," he called. "I bought some for all of us!"